Love,
Hopes, &
Marriage
Tropes

**The Romaine Wilder Mystery Series
by Abby Vandiver**

SECRETS, LIES, & CRAWFISH PIES (#1)
LOVE, HOPES, & MARRIAGE TROPES (#2)

Love, Hopes, & Marriage Tropes

A
Romaine Wilder
Mystery

ABBY L. VANDIVER

HENERY PRESS

To Kevin H. I would always choose you. L.A.A.Y.

ACKNOWLEDGMENTS

I always want to thank God first, my keeper and my friend. My mother who keeps Him company, as do my sisters. Thank you for all you've given me.

And a thank you to my publisher, Henery Press.

I want to also thank and give a shout out to my buddies at the South Euclid Lyndhurst Public Library. Bernard Francimore who is always full of ideas, and never too shy to share them with me. You inspire me. And Laurie Kincer, who epitomizes, and most times surpasses, the term librarian—knowledgeable and helpful, she can always put her finger on the right book or information just at the right time. Thank you for supporting me in my endeavors of becoming a better writer.

And of course, Kathryn. Couldn't do it without you, thank you sistah.

Chapter One

There was going to be a wedding at the funeral home.

I stood in a sea of rubrum lilies, mums, and baby's breath. Bubblegum pink taffeta bridesmaids' dresses with sweetheart necklines exposed more cleavage than any blushing bride should want her groom to witness, and short front hemlines uncovered perfectly tanned thighs.

And like everything in Texas the wedding was going to be big. A happy occasion, most everyone I'd seen that morning had been all smiles, especially my auntie. It would be her first time officiating a couple's nuptials. But the love in the air was suffocating me.

I wanted no part of it.

Unfortunately, the backyard of the Ball Funeral Home & Crematorium, the wedding venue, doubled as our family home—a renovated southern plantation—and I just couldn't seem to get around all the festivities. It was a beautiful setting if you were able to block out the dead bodies inside.

Trying to fix a bite to eat and brew a cup of coffee in my brand new Keurig meant I kept stumbling over wedding vendors, the photographer and the fighting flower girl and ring bearer.

I was definitely in the need of a caffeine fix right about now, and had purposely purchased the kind of brew master with pods so Auntie Zanne couldn't try to fix any of her "teas" in with the coffee grounds.

And before I could get a cup to my lips, I'd been pulled right into the thicket of things by one of the bridesmaids. J.R., our Jack

Russell terrier, watched at my feet without so much as a whimper as she wrapped her arm around mine and gave a yank. Dragging me with her, at the bride's request so she cooed, into one of the rooms off the kitchen hallway where the wedding party was readying for the ceremony. So far, though, I wasn't sure she'd noticed I'd arrived.

"Most people would kill to marry Bumper Hackett," the red-headed bridesmaid squealed as I made myself flush with the wall, hoping to make a quick escape. "Ain't that so, Tonya?"

"I know I would," Bridesmaid Tonya, who had grabbed me, admitted.

"Jorianne Alvarez," the first bridesmaid said. "You are so lucky!"

"Thank you, Marilee, but rest assured, I'd be the one killing somebody," the bride said, no hint of jest in her Texan twang. "Blood on my hands," she looked up toward the ceiling, "I swear to God, if anybody tried to take Bumper from me." She stood in front of the Cheval mirror and slid pink gloss across her lips. She smacked them to even out the color.

"That lil' ole Bumper bump you got there insured nobody else was gonna get 'em," Bridesmaid Marilee quipped. She nodded her head toward the emerging bulge under the soft tulle skirt of Jorianne's crisp white sheer-shouldered, silk and Chantilly lace wedding gown.

"You got that right," the bride said, she tossed the blonde ringlets from her face and held up a hand to be high-fived. "But that ain't nothing compared to the fire my momma set under him."

That sent her bridesmaids into a fit of giggles.

I shook my head. It was no wonder I'd witnessed the groom having panic attacks from the time he'd arrived. Inhaler in hand, short of breath, he was flush and feverish looking. A thin layer of sweat glistening across his forehead in the early morning sun and a constant cough, he'd almost run a rut into the lawn as he circled the backyard.

The make-shift dressing room was cluttered with duffle bags, curling irons, makeup, and clothes that the girls had changed out of strewn around the room. The light and airy scents of the flowers mixed with perfume filled the room and evoked jollity and a girlishness energy.

"Sugarplum," my Auntie Zanne said as she poked her head into the room. "We're gonna start soon, you getting the girls together?"

Added to her many other social excursions, Suzanne Arelia Sophie Babet Derbinay, christened as such by the Holy Roman Catholic Church, known by Babet to most, but Auntie Zanne to me was officiating and hosting.

I held up my hand. "Not my job. I was grabbing something to eat when one of them pulled me in," I said. Auntie slipped into the room and shut the door behind her.

"Oh, we almost forgot we sent Tonya after her," Marilee, the redheaded bridesmaid, chortled. She looked to my Auntie Zanne. "We wanted her to keep an eye on Bumper, Miss Babet. He's as nervous as a fly in a glue pot."

"It's his asthma," the bride said. She walked over to the window which faced the backyard where the wedding was going to take place, pulling back the sheer curtains she peered out. "It acts up when he gets nervous. Just look at him, poor baby." She shook her head. "He's been sucking on that inhaler for the last couple of days."

Marilee and Tonya moved to the window to take a gander.

"Maybe he should see a doctor," I said.

"Ain't you a doctor?" Marilee turned to me and said, a whole lot of accent and too much bite in her words. "*Doctor* Romaine Wilder, right?" She squinted an eye at me. "Or are you not a real doctor. Just one of them with letters behind their names?"

I decided not to even answer that comment.

"My momma ain't gonna let him outta her sight," Jorianne said, a smile beaming across her face, her bright blue eyes sparkling. "And that includes letting him go to the doctor's. She said he can go after we tie the knot."

"Unless he drops dead at the altar," the third bridesmaid said. She'd hadn't said a word until now. Standing in a corner brushing her hair and applying makeup, the short, thin bridesmaid had a quiet softness to her. Probably considered cute, she seemed mousy next to the stunningly beautiful bride.

The smiles on the other three girls' faces bottomed out.

"Piper Alvarez!" the bride squeaked. "That's my baby's daddy you're talking about. He's got to be around a long time for us."

"Then you had better learn to take care of him," Piper said. "He's not invincible, you know." Piper fingered her thin blonde hair.

"He's going to be taking care of *her*," Marilee said.

"You know he's going to the NFL," Tonya said. "As soon as he graduates from USC, and then Jorianne and her baby will have everything they could possibly want."

"I'm just saying," Piper said and shrugged. She spoke without looking at anyone, but didn't back down. Her petite, upturned nose and her brow wrinkled at the conversation. She ran her tongue on her dry, colorless lips. "Marriage is a partnership, you know."

Jorianne looked around the room then let a perturbed eye land on Piper. She walked over to her and plastered a fake smile on her face. "We just gotta get through today, lil' sis," Jorianne said. "I want my wedding day to be happy for everyone. Especially family. Maybe just today you can try not to tip over the outhouse. Okay? Can you do that for me?"

"Sure," Piper said and gave Jorianne the same bogus smile. "I can do that."

"Here," Jorianne said, handing her the tube of lip-gloss. "Put a little of this on. Give yourself some color." She turned around and walked back over by the window. I watched Piper lay the gloss on a nearby table without using it.

"And that's why I asked Dr. Wilder to come in," the bride continued, rubbing her hand over her stomach, she nodded my way. "She *is* a real doctor, Marilee. Miss Babet told me. And I was thinking that maybe she could do something to help Bumper." She looked at me. "Can you?"

"Sure she can, Jorianne," Auntie Zanne spoke for me. She wore her white hair tapered in the back and high on top. And playing her part to the hilt, she wore a clergy collar, black skirt, and low-heel black pumps. "She'll give him a once over." Then she grabbed my arm and pulled me toward the door. "And while she does that you girls finish getting ready. It's nearly time to get started." Auntie clicked her nail on her watch crystal.

"Right!" Jorianne squealed and jumped up and down, placing a hand underneath her belly. "Because I'm getting married!"

That brought laughter back into the room and gave us an exit. Auntie pulled me into the hallway and shut the door behind us.

"That boy's symptoms are probably due to him being at the long end of the proverbial shotgun," I said.

"Bonnie Alvarez doesn't have a shotgun, she carries a snub-nose, Smith & Wesson revolver, and I had her check it at the gate when she arrived, just like everybody else." Auntie Zanne took off down the hall back into the kitchen. "I won't abide by any shenanigans during my first time officiating," she said over a shoulder.

"This wedding isn't about you, Auntie," I said catching up with her in the kitchen.

"It's at my funeral home. My house. It's about me."

"How did they choose this place to have the ceremony anyway?" I asked as I grabbed a bottle of water from the refrigerator.

"I gave them a deal," she said matter-of-factly. "Discount on the arrangements for their great uncle who died last month if they had it here."

"Auntie," I said and chuckled. "That's despicable."

"That's business, darlin'." My Auntie Zanne had a special relationship with her dead clients—she talked to them and she believed they talked back to her. And she let everyone know about it, not worried in the least how crazy it sounded. "Plus," she continued, "Jorianne was happy to do it, it was one of my brews that sealed the deal with her and her little old high school sweetheart."

A look of semi-shock washed over my face. "She came to you for a love potion?"

"Why do you say it like that? A lot of people do."

"You shouldn't put such nonsense in young peoples' heads. You and your magic, hocus pocus."

"Pshaw!" She waved a hand at me. "It worked, didn't it?"

"Auntie," I said, speaking to her as if she were a child. "It might have had to do with her being pregnant. You ever thought about that?"

"Lots of people get pregnant," she said. "How many of them get married?" She raised her eyebrows. "This ain't 1958, kiddo." She pushed up next to me and rubbed my back. "You should pick out a guy for me to give a cup to." She gave a firm nod. "You might be the next one standing at the altar in front of me."

"That will never happened." I rolled my eyes.

"What? You'll never get married?" She covered her heart with her hand.

"You marrying me," I said. "I'll get a real preacher for that." I patted her on her cheek. "And, I'm steering away from this whole thing. I'm on my way to the new ME's office. I've got a delivery I can't miss."

"You're not staying for the wedding?"

"No," I said.

"I was hoping you could help me coordinate," she said, giving me a pout. "I just finished speaking with a family up front, and I need you to keep an eye on the business while I was marrying the happy couple."

"You're speaking to grieving families about funeral arrangements at the same time you're hosting a wedding?" I asked, disbelief evident in my words.

"Well ..." A sheepish look on her face. "I hadn't scheduled any appointments, but did you see how many people are coming up that driveway to go out back to the wedding? Hundreds," she said and took a peek out of the kitchen window. "I left some of my brochures for our burial plans out. People can only hope to get married. Death, my dear, is a sure bet. I have to sell our place of business whenever I can."

"'You left the brochures out? As in "out" at the wedding?"

"No silly," she said. "At the end of the drive, when the guests first come through. Very tastefully presented."

I bucked my eyes. "Oh yeah. That *is* better," I said hoping she'd catch the sarcasm.

"I know, genius right?" She smiled, telling me my disapproval went right over her head. "Now when the guests enter the yard they'll see what we have to offer."

"I have to go," I said, no need having this conversation with her. She saw no wrong in her actions. "So, I won't be here. Why don't you get your receptionist Floneva to speak to any would-be clients of yours?"

She shook her head. "Last time I saw her she was chasing the caterer trying to get samples. That woman eats like a horse."

"Babet!" Miller Alvarez, the father of the bride stepped through the back door and took off his tan-colored Stetson. "Bonnie says you're burning daylight and she's all over me to get this dang thing started."

"Wedding's not supposed to start until eleven thirty," Auntie Zanne said, looking down at her wristwatch. "And that's not for another fifteen minutes."

"What does it matter?" he said and swiped his fingers on either side of his dark brown handlebar moustache.

"It matters because you're supposed to get married with the hands going toward the hour," she said. "We wouldn't want to mess things up for those two before they can even get started."

Mr. Alvarez looked down at auntie from his six-foot-four, lanky frame and shook his head. "That boy is about to faint out there. You seen him? He might not last another fifteen minutes."

"He'll be alright," Auntie Zanne said. "Romaine's gonna have a look at him."

"Look. Can't you just talk slow?" he said and ran his hand down the side of his corduroy pants. I knew he had to be hot. No wonder he wanted to get started. "Then by 11:31 you'll be pronouncing them. You'll be happy. Bonnie'll be happy. That'll work won't it?"

"Oh heavens," Auntie said.

But before she could finish telling him her thoughts, he'd given me a once over and shook his head. "And I don't think my Bonnie Belle is gonna let anybody near that boy. Nobody but you and the bride until this thing is done."

Auntie flapped her arms on her sides, exasperated and looked from me up to the bride's daddy. "Okay," she said with a huff. "Let's do this." She pushed on Mr. Alvarez's arm. "You. Out. Romaine. You get the girls moving then standby to give the groom some doctoring once he's hitched."

There was always so much going on in this house. I knew I should have gotten up and left before daylight even hit.

"Girls," I said swinging the door open, reluctantly following my Auntie's orders. "The wedding is getting started." I pointed toward the window. "Time to head on out."

"Arrghh!" Jorianne said. She fanned her hands over her face. "I've got bees buzzing all over me," she smiled, "They're making me hot and nervous."

"It's okay," Marilee said and moved close to her friend. She'd filled her red hair with baby's breath and her eyes with a pound of mascara. "You're the first of us getting married. It's making us all nervous. It's just so exciting. I think I'ma cry." Her voice went shaky.

"Don't cry!" Jorianne said. "Then I'll start crying."

"Me too," Tonya chimed in and went over and made a circle with her friends. "And we'll mess up our make-up."

"Oh for Pete's sake," Piper said and grabbed a bouquet off the table. "I'm outta here if you guys drop one tear. Just let's please get this over with."

"I have to put my veil on," Jorianne said, shooting daggers at her sister.

"I'll help you," Marilee said. She tried to take the finely netted headpiece from Jorianne.

The bride swatted her hand away. "You're shaking like a leaf on a tree. You'll mess up my hair." She looked at me. "Dr. Wilder can you help me?"

"Sure," I said. "But we've got to hurry." I pulled the sheer curtain back and draped it over a nearby chair. Auntie Zanne, the groom and his best man, evidently a soldier dressed in a military uniform, were already standing under the flowered archway. The seventy-something organist, dressed in as much white as the bride, kept glancing toward the house expectantly, a plastered smile on her face, she was swaying and I hoped she'd still be upright when it was time for the Wedding March to be played. "Look. They're all ready to go." I nodded toward the scene outside the window, signaling for her to take a look.

"Ooooh!" she squeaked. "Okay. Okay. Okay! I'm ready." She handed me the veil and turned her back to face the window. I came up behind her, but she could hardly stand still, her legs going back and forth like a jump rope in double Dutch, head bobbing.

"You'll have to be still," I said.

"Okay," she said breathily. "I'll try."

"Just take deep breaths," I said, "and keep your eye on your groom." I put my chin over her shoulder, almost cheek-to-cheek and pointed.

But as I did, we both witnessed him do a violent body shake that made a surprised look flash across his face. Then his eyes went blank. Bumper coughed a couple of times and turned as pale as a ghost before he went down and collapsed into a heap.

"Oh Jesus!" Jorianne screamed. She hiked up her dress and ran for the door.

"Somebody call a doctor!" Marilee screeched as she ran behind her.

I guess the "letters" behind my name weren't good enough for her.

Chapter Two

"I'm a doctor."

A bevy of wedding guests had gathered around Bumper Hackett after he fell. Without lending help, they all stood around and gawked.

"Excuse me. Excuse me, please. I'm a doctor. Let me through."

I thought I was the only doctor in the house. That voice told me I was not.

Who was that other doctor?

It couldn't be...

I stopped walking and turned my ear toward his voice.

"Excuse me," he said.

Oh, he sounded familiar. Very familiar.

I knew it wasn't anyone from around Roble. That voice didn't have one ounce of Southern in it.

"I can help," he said, his voice low but strong.

He was someone I knew. Yes. Someone I knew *well.*

"Someone tell me what happened," he said.

Smoky and deep, the sound of that voice made the hair on my neck rise.

It made my heart flutter.

"Breathe," I said.

The backyard at the funeral home was large. Wild colorful perennials grew tall in an array of colors, a bouquet of fragrance filling the air. The gazebo sat to the back of my Auntie Zanne's white framed greenhouse. Surrounded by oceans of vibrant blooms of annuals, a rambling pebble stone walkway staggered its way down to it where it was bordered by a small pond. Auntie had borrowed a pair of swans from the Houston Zoo that swam lazily in the blue water where magnolia blossoms floated.

Auntie thought they were perfect symbols for the nuptials. Swans because they mate for life, and magnolia flowers because, so she contended, they were older than the birds and the bees.

A perfect place for a wedding.

A bad time for an emergency.

Piper had put her bouquet down and with a roll of her eyes plopped down in a chair. I had run to the kitchen and picked up my medical bag, but by the time I got down to the gazebo, I had found someone else was tending to Bumper's needs.

I stood on my tiptoes to see over the crowd, still I couldn't make him out. I was hesitant to push my way through, the groom already had help and I wasn't sure I wanted to know who that voice belonged to.

"Please everyone." The voice was coming from low to the ground now. "Stand back," it ordered. "Someone tell me his name."

"Bumper," I heard a sobbing woman answer.

"Bumper, can you hear me?" A hush had come over the crowd of guests and I heard the palm of a hand slap wet skin. "Bumper, open your eyes. Can you talk to me?"

"He's my son. That's my son," that same woman spoke through her tears. "His name is Michael. Michael Hackett, Jr, but he's my Bumper."

"Bumper! Bumper!" Jorianne screamed, echoing his mother's words. She had torn her way through the crowd and by the sound of her footsteps was stomping on the wooden floor of the gazebo. "Oh please, no! Don't let him die."

"That's my plan," the voice said calmly. "I need someone to call an ambulance. Now."

I stood still as a pack of people began to push past me. My feet wouldn't move and a foggy haze seemed to crest over me, the sun lost behind a cloud darkening my surroundings had made me feel disoriented. I closed my eyes to steady myself.

It couldn't be...

"And could someone get the... um... bride," the voice said. "Ma'am, you're going to have to let me work."

"I'm not a *ma'am!*" Jorianne cried. "I was supposed to be." She let out a wail. "Today. I was going to be a ma'am today."

"Come on, Jorianne." I heard gentleness in Tonya's voice. "Let's get out of the way. Let the doctor help Bumper."

"Call 911," another voice called out, repeating the doctor's request. "Call them now."

"I'm already on it." That was a voice I recognized. It belonged to Mr. Alvarez, the bride's father.

"Daddy!" Jorianne seemed to just notice him, her voice rushing behind her as she left the covered area. "Oh, Daddy, what is going on?"

"Jorianne, I can't call and get help if you don't let me go." His tone was rushed. Irritated.

"He has asthma," Bumper's sobbing mother said. "He's got an inhaler. Somewhere." Her voice was trembling. "Wait..." I heard her hesitate. "I have one in my purse."

I now noticed two groomsmen, tall enough to rise above my blocked view of the downed groom and the doctor who came to his aid. Dressed in matching tuxedos, one white, the other black, both looked lost—teary eyes wide, jaws slack, but somehow the word "inhaler" seemed to jolt them.

"I got one," one said. He was the thinner of the two, but still stocky. Six-foot-two at least, he was dark-complexioned and wore his shoulder length hair in dreads, falling neatly around his face.

"I've got one, too," the other said, choking out the words. It seemed he was trying to keep himself from crying.

"I've got one!" the bride said loudly, seemingly not to be outdone. "It's in my bag. Oh!" Panic rang through her words. "It's back in the room!" She started bawling again. "I can't get it! I can't leave him! I can't leave Bumper!"

"He's not breathing," the doctor said. Smooth and even. His

words strong as he took charge. "An inhaler won't be of any use. I'm going to loosen his bowtie and shirt." I could hear his voice judder as he moved the body, grunting sounds accompanying the actions he'd announced. "I have to start CPR."

"Oh my lord, please don't let anything happen to my baby! Oh!" Momma Hackett wailed, "You Alvarezs are killing him. Making him do this. Oh Jesus, help me! Somebody help my baby!"

"Everyone stay calm," the doctor ordered. "Someone please, can you help this man's mother."

"Bumper! No!" Jorianne shrieked.

She evidently wasn't getting enough recognition.

"Get her a chair," a stray voice said. "Get her into a chair before she hits the ground."

Then I heard, "Who? Jorianne or Miss Hackett?"

Voices were coming from everywhere. "What happened to him?" someone whispered. "Can you die from an asthma attack... Oh my, that poor woman..." I heard the murmurings.

A new voice chimed in. "Here, I've got a chair for Miss Hackett."

"Sit down, Jorianne," her father instructed.

"I don't have a chair," she bawled. "No one's gotten me a chair!"

"There's plenty of them around," he said. "Where's your momma?"

"I've got a chair for her, Mr. Alvarez." That was Marilee, I knew her tone.

"Doc." Mr. Alvarez's boots clacked as he walked onto the platform. "The dispatcher said an ambulance is on the way."

"Romaine!" I heard my name. "Make way for her. She's a doctor." The sea of congregants parted, I blinked and looking up on the platform of the gazebo, I saw my Auntie Zanne beckoning for me. "C'mon, Romaine. Come up here."

And that's when I saw *him*.

My ears hadn't deceived me.

Nor had my heart.

Chapter Three

Alexander Hale. The man I had prayed to come from Chicago and rescue me from my exile to Roble was bent over the limp and unconscious Groom Bumper administering CPR.

I hadn't seen him in nearly four months. My knees buckled and I wondered if the paramedics would be able to tend to two bodies. I was sure I was going down at any moment.

"C'mon," Auntie Zanne said and marched down the two steps and over to me. She grabbed my arm and started pulling me. Looking back at me, she said, "What is wrong with you?" I didn't answer. I couldn't. "And where did *he* come from? Your Chief-of-Staff."

I shrugged, shaking my head.

"Hi Romaine," Alex said, a half grin on his face as we arrived up the gazebo steps. Breathing hard, he pumped steady, even compressions, not missing a beat even when saying my name.

I threw up a floppy hand but couldn't form a response. My mouth had gone dry. Butterflies were doing the jitterbug in my stomach.

My Dr. Hale *had* come to the rescue, albeit for the groom. But he was there. In the flesh. He stopped pumping, leaned over Bumper and in one swift movement, tilted the head back and lifted his chin. Holding Bumper's nose between his fingers he pushed through two rescue breaths.

"Your Chief-of-Staff needs help," Auntie said to me. She'd said when she first met him that I never called him by his name. That I always referred to him by his title. Her saying it now was a way of showing me her dislike of him. I wasn't going to give in to her digs.

And, I knew better than to jump in during someone giving CPR unless asked. Doing that, disrupting counting or rhythm, could cause a critical mistake, but I stood ready if he did need me.

Alex leaned in and listened for breathing, there must not have been a response because he started his compressions again. "One and..." He looked at us. "Not me," he said panting, his words in the same cadence as his count. "I don't need help. Not right now." He looked at me. "Count."

"And seven and eight and nine and..." I had mentally been counting with him, standing over the two of them, I picked up where he'd left off.

"Romaine can take over for me if the paramedics take a while to get here," Alex said to Auntie Zanne. "If I get tired. How far away are they?"

"I'm not sure. Probably about fifteen minutes. No longer than that," she said. "Especially when they hear it's at my place."

Alex smirked at the comment. "I can go that long," he reassured her with a nod.

"Twenty-seven. Twenty-eight. Twenty-nine," I said a little louder, letting him know how close he was to switching up.

"Thirty," he called back and leaned in for another set of rescue breaths.

I looked around. "We need to get these people out of the way," I said, now drawn into the emergency, I shook off my anxiousness. I was an M.E., I didn't do rescue, by the time people got to me there was no hope of that, but I could handle myself in an emergency situation.

"Alex can take care of him," I said to Auntie Zanne, emphasizing me using his name and not his title. I looked at him as he counted. "If he needs me, I'll come back. Right now we need to get these people out of the way. The paramedics will need a clear path."

"Okay," Auntie Zanne said. "I'll get the Roble Belles to help me. Probably best for everyone to just go on home, don't you think? There won't be a wedding today."

The Roble Belles were the booster club for Roble High School's football team. Four of their five members were sixty-five and older. Flannery Poole, the youngest, was in her late fifties.

"Get whoever you need. Do what you think is best," I said, surveying the crowd, coming up with a plan to move them in my head. "I'll work my way to the front, moving people out the way so I can direct the paramedics to the back."

"What if your doctor needs you?" she asked and pointed toward Alex.

"He...He's not *my* doctor," I said, stumbling over my words, even though I had just called him that. I closed my eyes momentarily and shook my head. "I already said, if Alex needs me, Auntie, send someone for me. I'll just be in the front."

I stepped down from the gazebo, people instinctively moving aside to let me pass, their questioning eyes searching mine for answers. I saw anxious tears flowing when it should have been champagne. I nodded and put on the funeral face my auntie had taught me after I'd come to live with her and became part of her business. It was one I had continued to use often with families during the identification process as a Cook County medical examiner.

I made my way down the long and wide drive, asking people to clear a way for the paramedics, saying "not yet," when asked had they arrived yet, and keeping an ear open for word whether Alex needed me to relieve him. As I moved through the crowd, I was able to match some faces to the voices I'd heard.

Jorianne, the weeping bride, was surrounded by her bridesmaids and comforted by Mr. Dreadlocked Groomsman. Sitting beside her, he held her hand and directed others to give her more tissue from a box Marilee was holding. I scanned the anxious faces and her sister, Piper, was nowhere in sight.

The other groomsman stood guard over Mrs. Hackett. Oversized and solid, he had a ruddy complexion, arms that stuck out to his sides, unable to make them flush with his muscular body. His red-tinged eyes were blue, and his hair cut so short he looked nearly bald.

Delores Hackett, who I remembered from one of Auntie's many club meetings, although I hadn't seen her in a while, looked unsettled in the white folding chair. Sobs somewhat subsided, she sat shoulders slumped, the heel of her foot tapping to her racing apprehension. She swiped her nose and dabbed at her eyes with a balled up, overused tissue.

I backtracked. "May I?" I said to Marilee and pointed to the tissue box.

"Sure," she said and held the box out toward me.

I plucked out three and walked over to Mrs. Hackett. The groomsman reacted to my arrival, standing up straight, shoulders back, he seemed on alert, ready to pounce if I'd come to disturb. But as soon as I got close, Mrs. Hackett grabbed me.

"Is Bumper going to be okay?" she asked. Her eyes pleading.

I knew better than to give any definite answers.

"Dr. Hale is one of the best doctors I know."

"I remember you, though it's been so long. Babet's niece. You're a doctor, right?" she asked.

"I am," I said and handed her the tissues. I didn't add what kind of doctor I was.

"His asthma just started acting up in the last couple of days," she said. "I don't know what triggered it. He hadn't shown any sign of it for so long. At least the past few years. I thought he'd outgrown it."

"Nerves," the groomsman offered.

Mrs. Hackett glanced at him. "Maybe Boone is right. Bumper was so nervous about all of this." She dipped her head toward the scene. "It was a lot."

"Getting married makes everyone nervous," I said and gave her an unfettered smile.

"He's going into his third year at the University of Southern California, you know," she said. "USC star football player, and star student, just like in high school." She nodded firmly. "Then Jori came with her news..." She started pulling the tissue I'd had given her apart, shredding them into pieces. "And her mother insisted..."

"I see," I said, then a polite pause before I continued, changing the subject. "I'm heading out front to look for the ambulance." I didn't want to get involved in blame pointing. "We're going to get him to the hospital just as soon as we can."

"Good." Her gaze drifted and she started rocking from side to side.

"Okay," I said and looked up at the groomsman, the one Mrs. Hackett had called Boone. "I'm going to go." He gave me a nod.

"If you see his father, will you send him back?" Mrs. Hackett said, coming back to reality and stopping me before I stood up.

"His father?"

"I called Mr. Hackett," Boone said as way of an explanation to me. "He's on his way."

"Okay," I said.

"I hope he makes it before the ambulance gets here," Mrs. Hackett said. "He didn't want to come to the..." her voice trailed off.

"I see," I said. It was a phrase I used frequently. It showed I understood and that I had no opinion. Grieving people don't like opposition, they just want an ear to listen to whatever it is they have to say.

I didn't know what the groom's father looked like. I only knew her because she'd been to the house. "I'll be sure to tell him where you are," I said and gave a reassuring smile.

"He'll be driving a green Saturn," she said as if reading my mind.

"Got it," I said. I patted her hand and stood up. As I turned to walk away, I saw Rhett. He seemed to be waiting for me.

"I came to the house expecting to see smiles and rice thrown everywhere," he said. "Instead it looks like a crime scene."

"I know," I said. "This definitely didn't turn out the way Auntie Zanne had envisioned it I'm sure."

"Where is she?" he asked.

"She's supposed to be doing crowd dispersion." I glanced around, but like Piper, Auntie Zanne was nowhere to be found.

"I can do it," he said. "Whatever she was going to do, I can do. I can help." He looked at me, his bespectacled light-colored eyes filled with concern as if I was the damsel in distress. He nodded. "I got you."

Rhett Remmiere had skin the color of honey and just as smooth. He was tall and well-built, a newly joined member of Auntie's funeral home staff, he just seemed lost to me. Always hanging out eating in our kitchen, available at Auntie's beck and call, I didn't know whether he had a home to call his own.

Supposedly a former, or maybe not so former (he was so secretive about it), FBI agent, he had shown no interest in the investigation of the murder of a man we'd found stashed away in our funeral home. Not forthcoming about his personal life, I found him to be too interested in mine. Wanting to impress on the love I had of my mixed-race, French Creole heritage, he'd always tried to show off his command of the French language (although I'd never heard him attempt Louisiana Creole), or show off his passion for the blues and zydeco music, sucking up to me by equating himself with my guitar-playing father.

I hadn't decided yet what I thought about him.

Although, I at times could get lost in his eyes. Even behind his wire-rimmed glasses, it was easy to be moved by how striking and attractive those specks of gold that danced and twinkled in his eyes were. Especially when he smiled.

"Okay, then. Yes. You help get these people started on their way," I said. "Thank you."

"No problem," he said and smiled. *Twinkle. Twinkle.*

I turned away and looked toward the front of the house. "I've got to go wait for the paramedics," I said. I had enough distractions with Alex showing up, I didn't need any more, especially from Rhett.

"Who's tending to the groom?" Rhett asked and glanced toward the gazebo. "I would've thought it would be you."

"Appears I'm not the only doctor around."

"Oh," he said. He tilted his head and narrowed his eyes. "Should I be worried?"

I chuckled. "About what?"

"Someone coming around and sweeping you away."

I took in a breath. A girl could only hope.

Chapter Four

I finally made it to the front of the house. Forget about moving *people* out of the way, I found that there were cars everywhere.

The funeral home had a good-sized parking lot on the north side of the building, and the overflow usually parked on the street. But there were cars parked on the grass, on the perimeter of the property and were double and triple parked.

I didn't know where or how to begin to clear them out.

"We're getting everyone out of the backyard," Mark said. She brought me out of my reverie and back to the task at hand.

"We're moving them to the front," Leonard and Mark, the seventy-something twins and members of the Roble Belles announced as they walked across the front lawn.

The girls, who'd changed their name to their father's soon after their seventeenth birthday when he died, were giving me an update. I wasn't sure how they were doing that when they weren't even in the back.

"I thought Auntie Zanne was having everyone go home?" I said.

"They won't leave," the twins said almost in unison.

They were identical in every aspect, even their thinking. I didn't think anyone could tell them apart, and listening to them, it sometimes seemed that they shared a brain. Identical flowered, button-down shift-style dresses covered their thin frames, pink scarves were tied around their waists and corsages were pinned to their lapels. Their mostly gray hair pulled back in identical buns.

"Everyone wants to wait to make sure Bumper is okay," Leonard said. "Chester and Flannery are helping, too."

I looked around and those two were nowhere in sight either. Hopefully they were in the backyard. Chester Young was the only male in the Roble Belles, but he was proud to wear their insignia on his group jacket. And Flannery Poole was Roble's first every beauty queen. Even in her fifties, she was beautiful, with her smooth skin, shiny black hair and emerald green eyes.

"Well, for him to be okay, everyone will have to be sure to make room for the paramedics to get to him."

"Yes, we know," they said together.

"We'll remind them," Mark said.

"And all these cars are in the way," I said. "I don't know what to do about that."

They looked at each other and then at the cars.

"Maybe we should tell Babet?"

"Where is she?" I said.

"Manning the armory," they said together.

How do they do that?

I didn't know what that meant, but it wasn't easy to miss that my task had just become that much bigger with having to get cars instead of people out of the way, and I didn't have time to figure out what they were talking about.

As I moved to the edge of the driveway to determine how deep the obstructing cars were, I saw Auntie Zanne, her five-foot-three frame too diminutive for me to initially see over the big trucks encircling the property. She had a line of people in front of her and was digging in a big box.

"I thought you were moving people out of the way," I said after making my way over to her. "And I hadn't realized all these cars were out here so we've got to get them moving."

"I'm doing my part," she said.

"And what is that?" I asked and peeked over into her box.

"I had a cache of weapons I had to get back to their owners if I wanted them to leave."

Her box was filled with guns. It appeared she was giving them back to the people she collected them from.

"And when Delores started yelling what the Alvarez's had done to her son and Bonnie Alvarez disappeared, I figured I better check on my stash," she said. "Hey! Get your hand out of my box. One gun per person." Her attention was diverted from filling me in to a man reaching his hand into her box. "I'm the only one passing these out."

"Auntie," I said. "That does not look like a good thing." I looked at her cache.

"You telling me. I didn't want a Hatfield and McCoy shootout happening around here." She looked at the man standing in front of her, he held his gun in his hand but hadn't moved. "Is that your gun?" she asked. He nodded. "Well, then, get! Next!"

I shook my head. "Maybe the paramedics will just be able to squeeze through the cars and people," I said.

"Don't worry," she said. "I've got the Belles getting people out and once people collect their belongings, it'll clear out fast. You'll see."

"Okay," I told her, but still decided I should try to find or create a clear path.

As I walked further down the street, I saw Piper for the first time. She was standing with the military-clad best man. He beckoned and started to walk my way.

"Hi," he said. "Piper told me you were the doctor."

"Hi," I said. I wondered why either one of them weren't concerned enough to be in the back. They had even left from close to the house. It had to be obvious to them that the groom's asthma attack was pretty serious.

Shouldn't they want to see how he was doing?

"I am a doctor," I said. "But not the one tending to your friend, in case you were worried about him." I raised an eyebrow.

He licked his lips and glanced back at Piper. "I am worried about him," he said. "I was thinking if you were up here, he must be okay back there and we were getting ready to start the wedding.

That's why I came over to speak with you."

"He's going to go to the hospital," I said. "The wedding probably won't be today." I guessed the Belles hadn't made it over to him yet either to give the news.

"Oh," he said and licked his lips again. He rubbed his hand over his butch haircut. "He's going to be okay though, right?"

"Everything that can be done for him here is being done. His mom is at the house—in the back, pretty upset," I added. "And the bride." I leaned to the side to look past him at Piper.

"Oh yeah. We know. I don't really know anybody," he said. "So I just thought I'd stay up here out of the way.

Just as I was about to respond, I saw a flash of red in my periphery. "Excuse me," I said. "I think I see the ambulance." I started to walk away and then turned back to him. "Maybe you and Piper can help me make sure the paramedics have a clear path to the back?"

"Sure," he said and shrugged.

Some best man...

Chapter Five

"Surprise," Alexander Hale, M.D. and new Roble hero, said. He jumped off the back of the ambulance and walked over to me with his low held arms outstretched. His light blue shirt unbuttoned at the neck was tucked inside a pair of gray slacks. His sleeves rolled up, his hands were sweating from being inside latex gloves. He had a mischievous grin on his face and that sparkle that had made me fall for him the first time I'd laid eyes on him.

All had calmed down. Their faces intense and not uttering a word, the paramedics arrived, wended their way through all the congestion, took a report from Alex on his condition and were now whisking Groom Bumper Hackett off to the Sabine County Hospital without one guest or vehicle getting in the way or trampled. Bumper looked bad strapped to that bed, CPR halted, they'd attached an IV and brushed his damp hair off his still sweat-laden face.

The EMS workers let the itinerate Dr. Hale intubate Bumper in the back of the emergency van before they left. Luckily that gave Bumper's father enough time to make it to the house, and he and Mrs. Hackett, driven by Boone because there were too shaken, followed behind in that green Saturn.

We were standing in the front yard, most of the wedding attendees leaving after the ambulance arrived. Only a few stragglers were hanging out. As Alex passed the loiterers, making his way to me, a few patted him on the back, mumbling their thanks for the good deed done.

Auntie's funeral home staff and the Roble Belles stood in a group, speaking low, concern etched in their faces as they watched the ambulance speed away, red lights flashing and siren wailing. But after Alex came my way, so did all of their attention.

"Alex," I said the one word in a whisper, my breath getting caught in the back of my throat. I guess I hadn't yet overcome the shock of seeing him. "What are you doing here?"

"I came to see you," he said. "Wandered toward the back with the stream of people when I arrived and found a wedding going on. Kind of stopped me in my tracks, though." He looked at me. "I was hoping it wasn't you getting married."

"If you kept up with me better," I said. "You wouldn't have to hope it wasn't. You'd know."

He hugged me then stepped back and looked at me. "You look different," he said, not acknowledging my grumbling. "Your hair? It's all... fluffy."

The humidity in Texas had taken its toll on my hair. Back in Chicago, I kept it straight as a rod. I didn't put chemicals in my hair—no need after flat irons became so efficient. Long, black, silky, it often fell in my face and swung with every head movement. But my natural 'do was curly and wild. Texas brought out the real me.

I ran my hand over my hair to try to flatten it.

"And are you wearing a darker shade of make-up?" He ran his finger down my face.

I took in a breath. I wasn't even wearing make-up, something I wouldn't ever do in Chicago.

"It's a tan." Auntie Zanne was good at making awkward moments even more so. She walked over, her motley crew trailing behind. "Lots of sun down here in these parts." She tweaked up the twang.

"It's a good thing you came along," Flannery Poole said, interjecting, unknowingly saving me. She slid up next to Auntie Zanne and put her hand on Alex's arm. She gave him a Southern welcome smile.

"Good thing, indeed. I think I may have saved the day," Alex said.

"Romaine could have taken care of it," Auntie Zanne said.

I smiled. "Good thing you did." I ignored Auntie's comment. "It is good to see you," I said.

He wrapped his arms around me, pulling me close. It seemed as if I'd passed his inspection and now he acted as if we were the only two in the yard. "I've missed you," he said.

"What's that on your lips?" I said and pointed.

"I don't know," he said, pulling his head back and touching his lips with his fingertips. "What is it?"

"Looks like crumbs."

He swiped his fingers across his lips and then rolled the residue between his fingers. "Maybe it was from the groom. When I did mouth-to-mouth." He looked down at it. "Something he ate back there," Alex said and licked his lips trying to clear off the remaining bits. "Ugh!" He made a face. "It's bitter."

"I don't think it was from the caterer," Floneva said. "That caterer wasn't letting anyone get a taste of anything. He said it was for the reception and couldn't be touched until then."

"She should know," Auntie Zanne said, then leaned in and lowered her voice. "Just like she should know that you never eat the food for the reception before the wedding even starts."

"I don't know about that," Alex said. "I have proof that that groom got a hold of food from somewhere." He ran his fingers across his lips again for good measure. "And I can understand why that caterer didn't want anyone tasting anything he'd prepared. It's awful."

"Yeah, I've got a bitter taste in my mouth, too," Auntie said and narrowed her eyes at Alex.

"Are you from Chicago?" Chester asked.

"I am," Alex said. "I came to see Romaine. Thought she might want to grab a bite to eat. I wanted to talk to her about something."

"She just ate," Auntie said.

"I did not," I said.

"You said you were in the kitchen getting something to eat."

I had said that, but I never did get the chance to eat anything. But I didn't want to go back and forth with Auntie Zanne looking like a petulant child in front of Alex.

"What do you want to talk to me about?" I asked, those butterflies starting their dance again.

A lopsided grin appeared on his face. "You'll see. When we talk. Might be something you like."

"Well if that ain't vague," Auntie said. "I've got something to help you spill all the beans."

"Excuse me?" he said, leaning toward her trying to understand what she meant.

"I need to get to the office," I interjected. I hadn't ever told him about Auntie's "side" job. I pulled my cell phone out of my pocket and checked the time. "I've got a delivery and I'm late. You want to come with me?"

"The office?" Alex cocked his head to the side and stepped back from me. "You've got a job down here?"

"Yes, she does," Auntie Zanne said.

"No, I don't," I said to her, then turned to Alex. "I don't have a job." I shook my head. "I just offered to help set up the new office for the County ME."

"Why did you do that?" he asked.

"The medical examiner died," I said. "He'd served as the ME for three counties for thirty years." I shrugged. "They just wanted a more updated facility for the next medical examiner."

"Which will be Romaine," Auntie Zanne said.

I smirked. "No it won't," I said.

"Mark my words," Auntie said.

I hated when she used those words. With all of her sixth sense, voodoo hocus pocus, it seemed she was never wrong when she spouted that pronouncement.

"Well, it's okay," Alex said. He looked down at his clothes and shuddered as if a shiver ran up his spine. "I need to get cleaned up anyway. What about dinner? Then you can tell me all about your 'job.'" Alex chuckled.

"Okay. I can do that," I said.

He blew out a breath. "I'm going to have to find a room for the night and get cleaned up."

"For the night?" Auntie Zanne asked before I could. "You're staying for just one night?"

Alex put on a wide grin showing beautiful white teeth. "It's good to see you again, Mrs. Derbinay."

He was steering away from her nosiness. That was almost an impossibility. Whatever she wanted to know, she'd find out.

"Same here," Auntie Zanne said, not one bit of sincerity in her voice. "So what did you say brought you here?"

"I didn't say," he said. "But I've got a conference in Lake Charles starting tomorrow. Series of seminars." He looked at me. "I was hoping that Romaine would go with me. You can't attend most of them, but we'd be able to spend some time together."

"She can't go. She has a job," Auntie said.

"Will you stop with the job?" I said. I glanced around and noticed everyone staring at me. "How about we do dinner around five?" I asked. "It'll give me time to finish up over at the office."

"That sounds good," he said.

"You need me to pick you up?" I asked.

"No," he pointed to a Jaguar. "I flew into Louisiana, but got the rental so I could come and see you. I can meet you here. If that's okay with your aunt." He gave Auntie Zanne one of his winning smiles. I'm sure it didn't score one point in her book. "Then we can ride together."

"Okay," I said and smiled. "Sounds good."

Chapter Six

I had been evicted from my life.

All the things that had separated Alex and I in the first place came swirling into my head as I drove over to the new M.E. office to start on the autopsy. I got Auntie's permission to borrow one of her cars, all the while hoping she couldn't detect how befuddled I was over a man.

I remembered the moment I'd found out that cuts made to balance the Illinois budget had handed down my future without me having one say in it. It had made me feel off-balance. I was out of a job when the governor's defunding of services meant downsizing the Medical Examiner's office where I had worked for seven years, and I was too leery of what my finances would be in the coming year to renew the lease on my expensive Sheridan Park apartment in Uptown Chicago. Not wanting to dip into my nest egg, I decided to move.

My Auntie Zanne came up to see about me and persuaded me to come home. Back to Roble. A small town, population 985 including me, in East Texas.

That hadn't been the first time my Auntie Zanne had come to my rescue. At the tender age of twelve, I lost both my parents in a car accident. Auntie Zanne, my mother's oldest sister, high-tailed it to Beaumont where I lived to get me, arriving before I could shed a tear.

I pulled into the parking lot of the building housing the new medical examiner facilities. My deliveries, which were being made by Catfish, were scheduled to arrive any minute but I couldn't pull myself out of the car. Alexander Hale's appearance had sent me for a loop.

What did he want to talk to me about?

Maybe he was finally coming to tell me that everything was okay. That we could finally be together...

I closed my eyes and leaned back on the headrest. Maybe I could get back to the life I wanted.

Life had been different for me after coming to live with Auntie Zanne. She had been widowed at an early age and it had made her fiercely independent. She'd abandoned our French Creole heritage and turned Texan. Big hair and attitude, small town nosiness, she'd traded a Roman Catholic mass for a three-hour service at the local Baptist church, and abandoned her native Louisiana Creole language for a Southern drawl. The only thing she held onto from her roots was the magic and mystery of Voodoo.

I, on the other hand, was proud of my heritage, and that difference in us, even though we got along and I knew there was nothing in life she loved more than me, always made me want to leave. Forge the life I wanted some place other than there.

It hadn't ever been my intention to make my move back to Roble permanent, although Auntie told everyone I was there to stay. My plan was just to stay long enough to regroup, use my Chicago contacts, including Alex, to find another job. I'd be back in to the Big City in no time.

So I thought.

I soon found that the people I had included in my small circle of closest and dearest friends—the privileged and professional—became obtuse and aloof once my circumstances changed. But even with that fact swimming around in the back of my head, I didn't want to stay in Roble.

And I had been sure to let everyone in town know that.

I was going back to the life I had meticulously built for myself, which didn't include the familiar slow drawl and friendly countenance, colorful sayings, or intrusive hospitality of East

Texans. Nor did it include a weather forecast which included predictions on the amount my hair would frizz.

Something that didn't take long for Alex to notice.

Some may consider it rebelling, most thought it uppity. And at forty-something, it perhaps did seem quite childish of me, I know. But I didn't care. I just wanted something more, and I didn't want to count on Auntie Zanne again to give it to me. It was me that was supposed to be taking care of my eighty-two-year-old auntie. Not the other way around. It was me, after eight years of post-secondary education, and many more getting certifications, residencies, and fellowships who was supposed to move forward and not backward in status.

To have all the things my heart desired.

Which brought me right back to that bolt-out-of-the-blue—Dr. Alexander Hale.

The man who had saved the life of the groom.

The one that was hopefully all set to save me.

From the moment I met him, it was him that I dreamed of being with until death do we part.

But things don't always go the way one hopes. Alex turned out to be already married.

Separated. *Almost* divorced. So he put it.

But like one of those Southern sayings I wanted no part of, "almost" only counted in hand grenades and horseshoes.

Knock. Knock.

Knuckles hitting my window gave me a jump. It was Catfish. I pushed the switch and let down the window.

"I didn't hear you come up," I said. "You scared me."

"You were lost in thought," he said and smiled. "Unlock the door," he said, pointing at it. I popped it and he grabbed the outside handle and opened the door for me. He held out a hand to help me out. "I thought I'd beat you here with all the goings on at your house. You been here long?"

"You didn't hear?" I asked, stepping out of the car.

"Hear what?" he said.

"Groom had an asthma attack," I said. "Ambulance had to come and get him. They had to postpone the wedding."

"Oh wow," Catfish said. "So Babet didn't get to perform her first wedding, huh?" He laughed. "She was really looking forward to it."

"She'll get her chance. They'll probably only keep him overnight. Maybe they can try at another ceremony next weekend," I said. "If they do, though, I'll have to find someplace else to be."

Maybe in Chicago with Alex...

"I don't know," Catfish said. "Next week is Homecoming at the high school. She'll be super busy. Probably won't want to do another wedding then."

"That's next week?" I asked. "I will definitely have to be somewhere else."

In East Texas, football was next to God. And at a Roble High School Homecoming more people came to participate than there were sinners in church on Easter Sunday. Everyone came to give their praise whether the team was winning or not. Week long events—dinners, dances, school spirit activities and of course the game. A big deal for Roble High School, an even bigger deal for The Roble Belles Booster Club, which Auntie Zanne proudly ran.

"She didn't tell me," I said. "I'm surprised she hadn't asked me to help plan it."

"She wanted you to get the work done here," he said. "Finish setting up 'your office' as she told me."

I shook my head. "It's not my office," I said.

He held up his hands. "Only repeating what she said to me."

"You didn't tell her you were helping me today, did you?" I asked. "I told her I had deliveries coming. If she knew they were just from you, she would have tried to make me postpone them and stay at the house. I used them as a means of getting away."

Catfish laughed. "Didn't say a word. I figured if you wanted her to know, you would've told her."

"Thank you, Catfish," I said.

"Anything for you," he said.

Catfish looked cute in his green bucket hat and overalls, his usual attire. He was an outdoorsman, keeping property out in the pinelands close to the Sabine River. He fished, hunted and farmed, but he was handy and could help me with anything I needed.

He always kept his curly hair cut close and tapered on the side. He had stubbly five o'clock shadow all day and bright hazel eyes and caramel-colored skin. He'd had a crush on me from the day I arrived in Roble. Self-appointed guardian of the uppity black girl who thought she was French. He made sure no one bothered me and I got to grieve over the loss of my parents in my own time.

Although I couldn't ever see myself dating him, he was a good friend and I cared very much for him. I was just as protective of him as he was of me.

"Well, let's not stand in this parking lot all day," I said. "Let's see what you've got on this truck."

"I got it," he said. "You go on in and unlock the door. Can you prop it open for me?"

"Sure can," I said and smiled.

The new ME facility was up-to-date, well-lit, and beautiful. It made me beam with pride. I had been the point person for the County on style, design and functionality. Everything was state-of-the-art and had been ordered and installed by the contractor I chose and equipped with all of my suggestions. The County had been more than pleased with my work and was disappointed that I committed only to the design aspect of it all not taking the job.

I didn't even hesitate when I told them no I wouldn't take the position as the Tri-County Medical Examiner. Dr. Harley Westin, long time ME and longtime friend of our family, would have been happy that I followed in his footsteps. It was his shoes that I stepped into when Roble had its first ever murder. A murder that put the Ball Funeral Home front and center. A fact not taken too well by my Auntie Zanne, especially since it involved one of her closest and dearest friends, Josephine Gail Cox.

Josephine Gail suffered from depression. It was something well understood and well-guarded by my Auntie. She cared for her friend when her bouts would incapacitate her like she was her child. They had been friends since I could remember, and it was Auntie who nursed her back to health after her stays at the mental hospital, sometimes after sessions of electro shock therapy. When Roble's first murder involved Josephine Gail, my Auntie took up the case without hesitation.

I had asked Catfish to help me with what was left at the old office, mostly paper files and personal equipment that Doc Westin had left, and a few pictures that I thought would look nice on the walls.

Doc Westin had boxes of old autopsy reports that needed to be scanned into the new computer system. A few boxes looked personal. Looking through those was a Catch-22. I didn't want to pry into his business, and was planning on giving his personal items to his widow, but I wasn't sure if those boxes also contained confidential information on deaths and cases he'd worked on. I surely couldn't take the chance that I passed on such sensitive information.

"So I heard Chicago was trying to swoop you back up," Catfish said, he pulled his hat off his head and sat down across from me. He had a twinkle in his eye

"What are you talking about, Catfish?" I asked, a chuckle ready to erupt.

"Your gentleman caller."

"Ha!" I said. "Where'd you get that word from?"

"That's what he is, isn't he?"

"I thought you didn't hear anything about what happened today."

"I didn't hear about the asthma attack, but I know that you had a man come in town looking for you. One driving a real fancy car."

I shook my head. Alex must have stopped and asked for directions or something. I swear, Roble was the capital of Rumor Town.

"A red Jaguar," I said with a nod.

"You leaving with him?"

I tilted my head, thoughts racing through my head, I didn't know what to say to him. It's what I wanted to do. All my hopes resting on me going back to Chicago and being with him had been the reason I refused to take Doc Westin's position.

And Alex had said he had something to tell me.

"Don't have an answer for that?" Catfish broke into my thoughts. "Or just not an answer you want to share with me?"

"I don't mind sharing with you, Catfish," I said and shrugged. "It's just that I don't have an answer for that."

My cell phone rang and saved me. I didn't want to wax emotional. I dug it out of my bag and looked at the screen.

"It's Auntie Zanne," I said. "What could she want?"

"When it comes to Babet, you never know."

"Hi," I said, swiping the ACCEPT icon.

"Got bad news," she said, never one to beat around the bush.

"What?" I said. My mind went straight to Alex. "What happened?"

"It's Bumper," she said. "He's dead."

Chapter Seven

I couldn't get into the house fast enough for Auntie. When she gave me the news, she asked me to come as soon as I could. She needed me.

I thought perhaps she was upset about Bumper's death. After all, she was club members with his mother, and the wedding and his subsequent death happened at her home and place of business.

"I know Delores Hackett is beside herself," she'd said. "She is such a recluse. I don't think she's ever left Roble and Bumper was her life."

"I'm so sorry to hear that," I'd said.

"That poor, poor woman..."

But as soon as I got home, I learned it wasn't concern for that "poor, poor woman." It was that she wanted me to hurry so I'd have time to cook up something for her to take with her over to the Hackett's house. I didn't understand why she just couldn't cook something herself.

"I didn't think you'd ever get here," she said, standing behind me, she had her palms in the middle of my back pushing me toward the kitchen. I guess I wasn't moving fast enough for her. "I need you to get something done before you start getting ready for your date with the Chief-of-Staff."

"Alex," I said. Now I understood why it was so annoying when I kept calling him that. She had chastised me about it enough. "Just call him Alex."

"Alex, the Chicago doctor?" Rhett asked, putting a silly grin on his face as soon as we emerged through the doorway. He was sitting at the table eating. I wondered why whoever had fixed him food, couldn't do the same for the Hacketts.

"Do you have a home?" I asked.

"I do," he said. "I just like the warmth and coziness of this kitchen. Family gathered together. Good food. Nice company." He winked at me.

"You know, I know that you call yourself flirting with me," I said.

"I hoped you'd notice," Rhett said, still smiling.

"I was wondering if she ever would," Auntie said. "Sometimes even with all her book knowledge, she's pretty dumb about stuff."

"I just don't know if it might not be a waste of your time," I said.

"Better stop sending all these guys packing, she said, "might not be any gentlemen callers left to come."

"All what guys?" I said.

"I'm usually pretty good at managing my time," Rhett said, I guess rescuing me from my auntie's comment. "And it seems as if I always have time for you."

"Aww that was sweet," Auntie said, a big grin on her face. "Wasn't that sweet, Romaine? He has time for you."

"Have you been drinking some of Auntie's brews?" I asked.

He chuckled. "I may have let her try one or two out on me."

"See. Now I understand. I'd steer clear if I were you, Rhett. She'll have you crowing like a chicken, or barking like a dog, dancing naked under the moonlight."

"Dogs or chickens can't go naked," Auntie Zanne said. "You might want to tame down on your hyperbole. Work on not trying to scare away my clients."

"How about if I just work on whatever it is you want me to cook so I can go out on my date with my beau."

"Is he really your beau?" Rhett asked, it seemed his jovial smile he'd worn throughout our prior conversation had disappeared.

"Last time I checked he was," I said. All the time those words were tumbling from my lips, my head was reminding me that I really didn't know the answer to that.

"Look at you, all gussied up," Auntie Zanne said as I came down the steps. "Haven't seen you in make-up since you left Chicago."

"That's not true," I said, although it probably was. "I wanted to look nice to go out, Auntie, so don't give me a hard time about it."

I still was feeling bad from when she said I was sending men away. I surely didn't want to do that, but I wasn't quite sure if I wanted to give up on Alex yet either.

I'd straightened my hair as best I could with the humidity the Texas' air was laden with and put on make-up—the two things Alex noticed different about me. After seeing him, I couldn't decide if it was him I cared about anymore or that he was my ticket back out of Roble.

I had on five-inch heels, a slimming black dress with a plunging neckline and a swing to my walk. With the way I looked, there was nothing to complain about.

When Alex knocked, Auntie made me go and wait in the parlor, as she liked to call it. In her conversations with me about dating she always hastened back to an earlier time using terms like "courting" and "gentleman callers." I was nervous about him seeing me. As soon as Auntie walked him into the room, it was easy to see that he wasn't feeling well.

"What happened to you?" I asked.

His lips and the tip of his nose had a red tinge to them. His face was contorted like he was in pain and he was rubbing his hand over his belly.

"Does your stomach hurt?" I asked.

"Not really," he said. "I feel..." he shrugged, "just kind of nauseated, but that is nothing compared to this." He put his fingers up to his lips and winced. "They're really painful to the touch."

"Then don't touch them," Auntie said.

"You look awful," I said, I saw his fingertips were red too as he put his hands down. "What happened?"

"I don't know," he said. "I took a shower, lied across the bed and must've fell asleep. When I got up to get ready to come and get you, this is what I saw in the mirror."

"Did you eat anything?"

"Nope. Didn't want to ruin my appetite. Oh wait, I grabbed a bag of pretzels from the mini-bar." He shrugged. "But that's it."

"You can't go anywhere looking like that," Auntie Zanne said. She walked over to him and pulling him down to her height by his shoulder, she held onto his chin and turned his head from side to side. "I've got something to fix that. Heal you right up."

She looked at me, a sly grin on her face, I knew she was waiting for me to protest. She'd been wanting to fill Alex up with one of her brews since the first time she'd laid eyes on him. I didn't know if would be a truth serum, or some kind of staying concoction, or possibly even a disappearing powder so my heart and mind would be free to love whoever she decided was best for me. I watched her sashay out of the room, not taking her eye off of me waiting for me to object. Any other time I would have opposed what she aimed to do, but tonight I was thinking, why not? I knew whatever she cooked up for him wouldn't hurt him, it might even help whatever had caused his reaction.

But I also hoped that it would make him tell me everything, or want me more, or maybe even feel as if he couldn't live without me. I just had to wait to see what she gave him.

Chapter Eight

"You're not going to let her feed me something that'll make me fall in love with the first woman I meet, are you?" Alex let out a guarded chuckle. After Auntie and my exchange, I had noticed how he had watched us. Funny, even when you don't believe in something, when confronted with it, it can make you think twice about the realness of it.

"What if that woman were me?" I asked.

"I'm already in love with you," he said and came over to me. I searched his eyes for something that would tell me his words were true, but I saw nothing more than the pain he was having from him being sick.

"Why don't you sit down?" I said. "There." I pointed to the loveseat. I followed him over and sat next to him. "I wouldn't worry about what Auntie is getting for you. She's got a healing touch. And she won't hurt you."

"Maybe we won't be able to go out to dinner," he said, his eyes questioning me if it was alright. "Today didn't turn out like I planned it. I thought we would spend it together."

"Don't worry about dinner. I completely understand." I raised an eyebrow. "It didn't go like anyone planned it," I said. "Bumper died."

"Bumper?" His face showed momentary confusion. "Oh," he said and lifted his eyebrows, "the young man I gave CPR to?"

"Yep," I said and nodded.

"How is that possible?" he asked. "He was having an asthma

attack, I intubated him. He should have been fine."

"I know," I said. "I guess it was just his time." I looked over at him. "When will it be our time?"

"To die?" he said, his eyes big.

"No," I said, smacking his leg. "Our time to be together."

He shifted his weight and turned to me. "That's one of the things I wanted to tell you today. At dinner." I thought I saw a small twinkle in his eye.

"What?" The word came out hesitantly. I was so afraid of what he might say.

"I'm divorced."

"You are?" I said. I shook my head. "I don't understand. When did that happen? You didn't even tell me."

"That's why I hadn't been in touch as much. So much going on." He took my hand in his. "I just couldn't... didn't get to you like I wanted to. But it can be different now."

"Was it painful?" I asked. "Divorcing her?" My stomach was jelly and my lips dry, I didn't really want to hear the answer, but I needed to know.

"No." Then he seemed to realize what I was saying. "Baby, I told you a long time ago, it was a marriage of convenience. Not love. Getting that divorce was hard, but not for the reasons you think."

"We'll soon find out what *you* think," Auntie walked into the room, interrupting our conversation, steam from the cup trailing behind her. "About everything."

Chapter Nine

Auntie and I went over to pay our respects to the Hackett family. I had the pan of baked spaghetti I'd cooked before getting dressed for my date with Alex, and we'd picked up a package of toilet paper and paper plates from the supermarket.

"People always bring food to the home of the bereaved," Auntie Zanne had said as she directed me into the grocery store parking lot, "because people come and stay all day. They have to eat, but no one thinks or prepares for the consequences."

Hence the other items.

Auntie handed me the car keys as we left the house, although I didn't feel like driving. I was still nervous about Alex—his health, his news, and what it all meant for me.

Whatever Auntie had given him, I noticed had made his eyes glaze over and his head seemed too heavy for him to hold up. I didn't know what I had been thinking—that he'd drink her tea and suddenly start talking, telling me every little thing my heart desired. I'd never believed in her potions, but this one time, way deep down in my soul, I'd wanted so badly for it to work. For it to help me look into my future and know what was waiting for me with this man.

Instead we put Alex in one of the back rooms off the kitchen hallway, the same room the bride and her attendants had used, before we left. He was lucid enough, but groggy and walked on his own accord to the room, my arm looped through his guiding the way. He didn't give Auntie one ounce of discussion about her request that he stay. She had an almost charmed way with people when she was working in her side "business." It was like a hypnotic suggestion from her, which he couldn't rebuff and seemingly gladly went along with. She had him lay on the bed, we covered him up and left. Auntie assuring me he'd be fine until we got back.

But on the entire drive over the Hackett's house, I thought maybe I should have stayed in case he had more to say. In case there was something he wanted to tell me.

Or had Auntie given him something that would stop him from telling me what I wanted to know...

Then I felt bad. It seemed I cared more about what he had to offer me than I did what was wrong with him... Geesh. I was definitely confused.

The Hackett house was small and worn, but neat. The grass mowed short. The bushes shorn evenly. No stray stones from their gravel driveway. The green Saturn wasn't anywhere in sight, but there was an amber glow coming through the drapes in the large picture window and silhouettes easily visible inside. Someone was home.

We walked up the wooden steps and Auntie Zanne knocked on the oak colored door. There was rumbling inside and I thought I noticed someone pull the curtain back and peak through the window.

"Hi." A young woman pulled the door open.

"Hello," Auntie Zanne said. "We've come to see about Delores."

"Oh. Okay. Come on in," the girl said pulling the door wider.

We stepped inside. "I'm Babet Derbinay," Auntie said, a solemn look on her face. "This is my niece Dr. Romaine Wilder." She pointed to me.

"I'm Gaylon. Delores is my aunt," the young woman said. "She's in the dining room." She reached out and took the covered dish from Auntie. "I can put this in the kitchen for you."

As we were passing through the living room, we saw the two groomsmen who had been dressed in tuxedos at the wedding sitting on the couch and Auntie stopped.

"Hi, Mrs. Derbinay," Mr. Dreadlocked Groomsman said. He was now dressed in a football jersey and a pair of jeans. He held onto a football that he tossed around in hands.

"Hello, LaJay," Auntie said. "Boone." Auntie nodded at the other one.

"Hey, Mrs. Derbinay," Boone said, his words dry.

"Y'all taking care of Mrs. Hackett?"

"Yes, ma'am," Boone said. "We're sticking close." He hung his head. "But it's hard on both of us, too."

"I'm sure it is." She gave them a slight smile. "Boone you've known Bumper since grade school, haven't you?"

"Yes ma'am. Kindergarten."

"Bumper and I've been friends since seventh grade," LaJay said. "And we were just as close."

"I remember," Auntie Zanne said and nodded. She paused momentarily before she spoke again. "Boys, this is my niece, Romaine Wilder." She pointed to me.

"Hello," I said.

"That's Boone Alouette and LaJay Reid," Auntie said, pointing to each one of them as she said their names.

"I remember you," LaJay said. "You're a doctor, right?"

"Yes, I am," I said. "And I remember the both of you. Boone, you were such a help to Mrs. Hackett today." I gave him a small smile. "My condolences to you both."

"Thanks," Boone said.

"Thank you," LaJay repeated the sentiment. Getting up, he stepped around the coffee table and came over and took the bag out of my hand. "I'll put this in the back for you." I guess he thought it was food. The niece had disappeared through the back of the house. They'd figure it out once they peeked inside.

"The boys all played football together for Roble High," Auntie Zanne said, turning to me. "All through high school. They were the stars during their JV and varsity years. And then they all went to Division I colleges. The Roble Belles were really proud of them."

She glanced at Boone and smiled. "Still are."

"We couldn't have done it without you guys," LaJay said, coming back into the room.

"I was just going to say that," Boone said and smiled. "They were the best booster club even though none of them were our parents."

"We always think of you boys as our own," Auntie Zanne said. "That's why I wanted to have the wedding at my place."

"I just wish that it had of turned out better," Boone said.

"Yeah, man, me too," LaJay murmured.

"We're going to go and say hi," Auntie Zanne said and pointed toward the dining room. "Give our condolences."

We rounded the corner into the dining room and found Mrs. Hackett sitting at the head of a long, plastic cloth-covered table. She looked like she had earlier sitting in that folding chair– helpless. Hapless.

There were people in chairs and leaning up against the walls filling the small room to capacity. Auntie zig-zagged and "excused" herself over to Mrs. Hackett. When she got to her she bent over and hugged the grieving mother, then holding on tightly, she spoke, her face nearly touching hers. "We came by to see about you, Delores," Auntie Zanne said.

"Babet," she mumbled, tears streaming down her face.

Two men, who'd been sitting at the table got up and gave us their seats. They went into the kitchen where the niece had disappeared and had yet to return.

"Hello, Mrs. Hackett," I said.

"We wanted to see what we can do for you," Auntie Zanne said. She touched her cheek to Bumper's mother's before she stood up and rubbed Mrs. Hackett's back.

"There isn't anything you can do, Babet," she said, her eyes lowered. "Or you." Her eyes only flickered my way. "Nothing no one can do now. I tried. Lord knows I tried to keep him safe and I couldn't." I saw a tear roll down her cheek.

"Keep him safe?" I said. She made it seem as if someone was

after him.

"She's talking about those inhalers," the niece said coming back into the room. She must have noticed the confusion in my voice. "She keeps talking about them." She squinted her eyes at us and barely shook her head, as if it wasn't a good subject to talk with her about. "Your lasagna looks good," Gaylon said, a polite smile on her face, I could tell she wanted to change the subject.

"It's baked spaghetti," I said.

"Really?" she said. "I don't think I've ever heard of that."

"I don't understand why they didn't work," Mrs. Hackett said, her eyes focused on a spot on the wall. She hadn't taken the detour off her topic with us. "I made sure everyone had one in case he needed it. Everyone was prepared to help. I think maybe they might've been too old."

"Too old?" I asked, the niece giving me a look of disapproval.

"They might have been expired," she said, but as she talked the niece was shaking her head as if to say her words weren't true. "I had a couple around the house. I always kept them handy. One in every room." Mrs. Hackett continued, not noticing her niece. "He hadn't needed them for so long..."

"You said earlier that being nervous is what triggered it," I said.

"It was usually triggered by changes in weather," she said. "High humidity. That's why I was so happy when he got that scholarship to USC. Weather's always the same there."

"Is that when his attacks stopped?" I asked.

"His asthma had practically disappeared," Gaylon said, reluctant, yet seemingly compelled to explain. "As he got older, you know. It was bad when he was a baby, but by the time he started playing football in the pee-wee league, he was over it. But no one could convince Aunt Delores of that."

"I had to protect my baby. You know when the humidity was high, sometimes it would still act up," Mrs. Hackett said.

"Yeah, but his body had adjusted to the humidity here," Gaylon said. She blew out a breath like she'd had this conversation a few times.

"And when he moved to California," Mrs. Hackett said, "they stopped all together." She sniffed back a tear, seemingly not realizing her niece was accusing her of overreacting to her son's ailments. "He was going to move there. No humidity there." She let out a weak attempt at a chuckle, but it came out more like a hiccup and brought on a flood of tears.

"Here, Aunt Delores," Gaylon reached for a box of tissues that sat in the middle of the table and gave her a couple. "It's going to be okay."

Mrs. Hackett reached out for the tissue and looked up at her niece, no expression evident on her face. "It's never going to be okay again," she said and dabbed at her face. "Not ever again."

"I wondered why so many people said they had inhalers yesterday," I said.

"That way, whomever he was with," Mrs. Hackett said, "if he needed it, he would have it." She ran a shaky hand over her face.

"And it made her feel better too," Gaylon said.

"I guess it could have been his nerves..." Mrs. Hackett's blank eyes looked at Auntie Zanne.

"It's alright." Auntie Zanne got up from her seat and went back over to stand near her friend.

I heard the door swing open, not having heard a knock, I figured it might be Mr. Hackett so I stood up to greet him. Murmurings of greetings floated in from the living room, and then around the corner came the last person I expected to see.

Piper Alvarez.

"Hi everybody," she said smiling, a big pot of something in her oven-mitt clad hands. She acted more like she was coming to a pot luck dinner than to show her respect. She walked over to Mrs. Hackett, bent over and kissed her on the cheek. "Jori couldn't get out of bed, so she sent me. Where should I put this?"

"I'll take it," Gaylon said. "Just let me get a dishtowel."

"Oh, it's not hot now," Piper said, she looked down at her hands. "It was when I left home."

"Oh, okay," Gaylon said, and grabbed the pot. "I've got it."

Piper, potless, leaned into Mrs. Hackett and rubbed her back. Mrs. Hackett looked up and produced a perfunctory smile. She reached out for Piper's hand but missed it and let it plop into her lap. Piper grasped it and gave her a squeeze. She stood up straight and glanced around the room.

"I can't stay long," she said, blowing out a breath like she'd been rushing around. She plopped down in a chair that had been vacated for her when she came in and smiled at everyone as her eyes circled the table. Her thin blonde hair pulled back into a ponytail, she was wearing blue jeans, and a Texas A&M t-shirt. "Just came to stand in for my sister."

I was surprised she'd do anything for her sister when it came to Bumper. She hadn't seemed too happy being at the wedding or, for that matter, in the wedding. And to top it off, when Bumper got sick, she was nowhere to be found.

"It was the least I could do," she was still talking. "I hated to tell her I told you so, but I'd been telling her that Bumper was not invincible. She was going to have to learn to take care of herself. And now look," she flapped a hand, "from here on out, she *is* going have to take care of herself. She's on her own. Maybe this will teach her a lesson."

Now that sounded more like the girl I'd met at the wedding.

Chapter Ten

The house had started to fill up with mourners. Friends and family members were walking around mingling, speaking softly, carrying on their various conversations. People were eating, drinking and every now and then you'd hear a laugh or chuckle, probably people reminiscing about Bumper.

But Piper's comment and connotation came in loud and clear, and everyone that sat close by stopped and looked at her

"What?" Mrs. Hackett for the first time let her eyes focus on someone. She squinted them, trying to focus on Piper so she could understand. She sniffed back her tears.

Gaylon's faced mirrored mine, the same surprised look when someone says something inappropriate and seemingly not even having a clue they've done so.

"We're going to go." Auntie Zanne said stood up, and taking over Gaylon's role as protector said, "And we're taking Piper with us."

"What?" This time the one word response belonged to Piper.

"Delores needs her rest," Auntie Zanne said. "And not so much conversation."

I stood up. Ready to go. Confrontation with the grieving I knew, just like Auntie, was not a good thing.

"Gaylon, you'll see us to the door?" Auntie gave a head nod to Mrs. Hackett's niece.

"Yes," she said, seemingly appreciative to Auntie Zanne for helping with Piper.

Auntie Zanne went over and gave Mrs. Hackett a squeeze. "I'll stop by and speak to you tomorrow." She gave Piper a once over. "Let's go," she said to her in no uncertain terms.

"I-I just got here," Piper said, frowning at Auntie Zanne.

"And somehow you've stayed too long," Auntie Zanne said. She gave Piper's shoulder a poke, prodding her to get up.

"I guess I've done what I promised," Piper said.

"And more," Auntie Zanne said. "C'mon we'll walk you to your car."

Gaylon followed us to the door. She gave Auntie a hug, I was sure it was a sign of appreciation. She'd evidently appointed herself Mrs. Hackett's guardian.

"Thank y'all for coming," she said.

"Where'd you park?" Auntie asked Piper once we'd stepped out onto the porch.

"Over there," she said and pointed to a big black truck.

"Good, that's my Cadillac next to it," we'll walk together.

"You're driving that big truck?" I asked. She was such a little thing, it looked as if it might swallow her up.

"Yep, that's my baby," she said. "And if you see us coming, you'd better watch out."

I'd thought Auntie Zanne was going to light into Piper once we got outside. She didn't take any nonsense especially when it came to the grieving family members. Instead, she held onto her arm and sidled up next to her.

"Who was that caterer your momma got for the wedding?" Auntie Zanne said. "Everything was so chaotic this morning that I didn't get a chance to get his information. I may need him for another event I'm having."

"Exquisite Caterers," Piper said, not seeming to notice Auntie's change in demeanor. "But my momma didn't hire him. The caterers were sort of a wedding gift from Bumper's coach."

"Coach Williams?" Auntie asked about Roble's high school football coach.

"No. His USC coach."

"Why did you say that was 'sort of' of wedding gift?" Auntie asked.

"Well, because you know coaches can't give gifts. It's against the NCAA rules or something. This caterer was his cousin or cousin's husband or something and he gave us a deep discount. Momma said it may as well have been free, which is how things always work out for Jori, things just fall into her lap. But..." Piper turned back and looked at the house, "we weren't supposed to tell Bumper about it."

"No?"

"No," she said. "So please don't mention it."

"Don't worry," Auntie said, "I won't tell a soul."

We watched as Piper climbed into her car and pulled out before we got into ours. I opened Auntie's car door and waited until she was buckled in before shutting it. When I slid into my seat, Auntie looked at me and shook her head. "That girl has lost her vertical hold. She don't know how to act."

I chuckled. "There is something wrong with her."

"No," Auntie said, shaking her head. "There's a lot wrong with her."

Chapter Eleven

And there seemed to be a lot wrong with Bumper dying.

Auntie's questioning of Piper about the caterer got me to thinking.

Something just didn't seem right.

I didn't know exactly what is was. Something nagging at the back of my mind, I just knew that I had questions, too. I thought about it the entire drive home, and was surprised when I pulled into the driveway and didn't notice Alex's rental was gone until Auntie took note of it.

"That's not good," she said.

"What?" I asked.

"We weren't gone that long."

"And what does that mean?"

"I gave him enough of that staying brew to hold him down much longer than this." That was the first I noticed there was no sign of Alex. "That means it's a pretty strong force inside of him that drives him," Auntie continued.

I rolled my eyes. "You and your concoctions." I shook my head. "I'm sure he just wanted to lie down in his hotel room. He wasn't feeling well."

"He felt well enough to leave." She raised an eyebrow at me. "Check your phone. Did you miss a call from him?"

"I'm not checking my phone," I said, slight indignation in my voice. "Can we just get out of the car?"

She shook her head in disbelief. "I don't think you'll be able to make that one sit still long enough to get him to the altar."

I got out of the car and left her sitting there.

As I headed into the small, tiled add-on entryway and up the few steps to the main floor, I turned to see where Auntie was then pulled my cell phone out of my pocket.

"No missed calls," I muttered and checked my messages. Nothing.

Where did he go?

And why did he leave without telling me?

I went straight to my room and found J.R. laying at the foot of my bed.

"Hey, boy, you waiting for me?"

He lifted his head, ears perked, but that was as far as he went. Didn't run to me or bark me out a hello.

"Don't have the strength to come greet me?" I said. "Must have lent some of it to Alex. Even being sick, he had enough energy to leave."

I slumped down into my computer desk chair, set my cell phone next to the keyboard to keep an eye out for Alex's call or text, and fired up my Dell desktop. J.R. must've mustered up enough oomph to move because he came over and laid at my feet.

The first thing I looked up was Bumper's Facebook page. He was so young, full of life and from what I understood had a bright future in front of him. I didn't have a Facebook account—social media just wasn't my thing—but his page wasn't private and it was no problem bringing up his profile page from the link after I googled his name.

There were oodles of pictures. I sat, clicking through and staring at each one. Bristling with life, he was all smiles in most of them. Happy. Eager. Animated.

Was the Alvarezs' plot to make their daughter an honest woman really making him so nervous that he had an asthma attack? Although, I wasn't sure if being nervous was a trigger. It even seemed as if Gaylon, a cousin who appeared close to his age, thought it wasn't as bad as his mother professed or I guessed it to be.

Mrs. Hackett hadn't seemed too convinced about his nerves being the cause of his asthma attack, although the entire time he was out back waiting for the ceremony to start that was how his demeanor struck me. Nervous. Worried. Enervated.

No, his mother had said his trigger was changes in weather. I clicked open another tab and looked up the weather report for the last couple of days to check the humidity. I knew it was doing a job on my hair, but a quick look showed me it hadn't been higher than any other day.

So that couldn't be it...

I clicked back to Facebook and scrolled down, studying his Timeline. A smiling picture of Jorianne in a bikini holding a drink on a beach was the first one I saw. *I can't wait to make this one my wife,* the post read. The next one he'd written his wedding date and the words, *a dream come true* underneath. The next picture was him, Boone, LaJay and a few other guys I didn't recognize. Wasn't even sure I'd seen them at the wedding. He posted they were at the Golden Nugget. *Countdown,* it read, *Until I'm Officially OFF the Market!*

Must have been his bachelor's party.

I clicked on *Photos.* More than two thirds were of Jorianne or them together.

"This looks less like a shotgun wedding, and more like a happily ever after kind of thing," I muttered. "Why would he be so nervous about something he was evidently looking forward to?"

I clicked through other pictures in his album. Pictures of his football days at Roble High, navy, gold and white uniforms and then shots of him playing at USC—his new colors cardinal and gold looking just as fit and happy as ever.

I drummed my fingers on the desk. Why was he having an asthma attack?

And why did it kill him?

I typed "asthma" into my browser and read what I already knew. Statistically, the web entries relayed, the number of people that die from an asthma attack is low. And something else I didn't need anyone to tell me, most times rescue inhalers more often than not do the trick. It relieves the symptoms. No need for further intervention. Bride Jorianne had said he'd "been sucking" on it for two days. So why hadn't it worked? Mrs. Hackett thought perhaps they were old and expired.

Old.

Old, she assumed must have meant they were no good. But not always. Medicines can lose their potency after a while, true, and that's why expiration dates are stamped on them. But old didn't necessarily mean ineffective. And so, maybe the one he had wasn't helping, but so many people had a "back-up" one for him that one of them should've done the trick. If he felt one wasn't working, why not get another one from someone else?

I glanced down at the phone. It lay silent.

How was I going to concentrate and figure out what was bothering me about Bumper's death if I couldn't keep my mind off of why Alex had left?

He had to feel better, I reasoned, no need to worry about that or else he wouldn't have left. Right? Thinking that made me feel better about only thinking of what Alex was doing to me.

Which was what?

Driving me crazy!

That's what. I slapped my hands down on the desk and hopped up. J.R. opened one eye and glanced my way.

Geesh! If Alex was feeling better, why hadn't he waited for me to get back? Taken me to that dinner he promised. Explained better what *his* divorce meant for *us*.

I sat back down and slumped in my seat. Maybe he hadn't gotten any better. Auntie Zanne was always trying to disillusion me, get me to see things her way because my way, so she said, wasn't the right way.

But I was the doctor and I just couldn't see anyone getting better that quickly. Although I didn't know what was wrong with him...

Chapter Twelve

Once I came to that conclusion, I knew I needed to call my cousin, Pogue Folsom. He was the sheriff in Roble and if my hunch was right, he was going to have to get on this right away. All of this spinning around in my head—thoughts of dastardly deeds, a person or persons doing away with someone at their wedding—had to be shared. I just hated to see Pogue go through it again.

Yep. We'd just got past one murder.

The very first murder in Roble's long, illustrious recorded history. Okay, so probably other than a zero-crime rate, there hadn't been much else to Roble's history but that, however, was changing fast. One murder at a time.

It hadn't even been two months since that murder and it too had entangled Auntie's business up in it.

When I moved from Chicago, Auntie Zanne had come up and spent the last two weeks with me. She'd hoped to make the transition easier on me, but it didn't help. I cried the entire train ride back, so disappointed that I was right back where I started. And things didn't get any better after we arrived.

Josephine Gail was standing in the rainstorm that had ushered us in. Soaking wet, she was waiting for Pogue to arrive. She wouldn't speak to us and it was impossible to get her out of that storm. Pogue had to fill us in once he got there. He told us that there was, according to Josephine Gail, an errant body in the funeral home. One, she determined, that had been murdered.

She was right.

The Annual Crawfish Boil and Music Festival was the backdrop for solving that murder. Now it looked like a wedding was going to be it this time.

I blew out a breath, picked up my cell phone and punched in my cousin's number.

"Hi Pogue," I said.

"Hi," he sounded groggy. I glanced at the time on the computer. It was later than I thought.

"Did I wake you?"

"Sort of. You alright?"

"Yep. But after I tell you what I have to say, you may not be."

"What Romie?" he said, his voice with a little more vigor.

"You're not going to like this."

"Like what, Romie? Can you just tell me?"

"You sitting down?"

"How cliché," he said.

I didn't say anything.

"Do I need to sit down?" he asked, seemingly exasperated with me already. "Because I am laying down."

"I guess that'll work," I said.

"Just tell me."

"Michael 'Bumper' Hackett's manner of death is probably homicide." I wasn't sure he knew who that was, but I had to give him the news.

I heard a long grunt come over the line. "Oh geez," he said. "Don't tell me there's been another murder."

"Sorry."

"I thought he had an asthma attack?"

"You heard about it?"

"Yeah, Momma told me," Pogue said. "One of her club members told her and ain't no telling who told them."

"Small town gossip train. That's how we found out, too. Someone called Auntie. When we put him into that ambulance, we—at least I—thought he was going to be okay."

"But just like gossip, they didn't have it all right, huh? Wasn't asthma that killed him?"

"Nope. I think he was poisoned."

"Poisoned? Wow." I heard him take in a breath. "What kind of poison?"

"I don't know. He needs to be autopsied."

"So then what makes you think that?" he asked.

"Because, his rescue inhaler would have helped him if it were asthma. Two days and a constant mist of albuterol should have done the trick."

"Maybe he needed something more."

"Like what?"

"Heck, I don't know, Romie. You're the doctor."

"His asthma was being managed. In fact, his mother said that he hadn't had an attack in a few years."

"Really?"

"Yes. And get this. After touching him, Alex's lips, nose and fingertips turned red and he became nauseous."

"Who is Alex?"

Oh yeah. He didn't know, although I was sure it wouldn't be long before my Aunt Julep got wind of that little rumor mill tidbit as well and bring him up to date.

"Alex Hale," I said. "The doctor from Chicago. Remember I told you about him."

"Oh my," he said, that obviously jogging his memory. "The would-be, almost-divorced man toy."

"Shut it," I said. "I never told you he was my man toy."

Pogue chuckled. "So, he's here? In Roble?"

"No. He did CPR from Chicago."

"Oh that's who did the CPR at the gazebo? I'd heard about that, but didn't know who it was."

"Obviously."

"So where is he?'

"He was here, but he left."

"And?"

"Long story. One I don't want to go into now."

"Okay then. Back to the alleged murder."

"Not alleged. Very real. At least I think so."

"Okay. So someone tried to poison Alex, too?"

"No," I said. My tone said that his suggestion sounded ridiculous. But I guess I hadn't done well so far in explaining the connection and I knew part of my irritation was him questioning me about Alex. "Some of the poison must have transferred when Alex gave Bumper mouth to mouth."

He was quiet for a few seconds, seemingly piecing together what I'd said. "Oh. I see. He got some of what poisoned Bumper?"

"Yep."

"What did Bumper eat? Did anyone else get some of the food? I heard it was like five hundred people there."

"More like a hundred and fifty. No more than two hundred." I shook my head remembering the crowd size. "I think that it wasn't in any of the food." I licked my lips, forming my thoughts. "Floneva said that the caterer wouldn't let anyone eat."

"What then, an injection?" he asked.

An injection... I mulled that suggestion over. If someone injected him with the poison, they had to be close enough to him to give him a shot. Through his clothes. And if that's the way it happened, then how did Alex pick that up?

Then it hit me.

"It was the inhaler," I said. "That's how he was poisoned. It has to be."

"Wasn't he using the inhaler to help with his asthma?" he said.

"If I'm right, that's what makes this so sinister," I said. "The same thing that was supposed to save his life was the instrument of his death."

"That is terrible."

"Whatever kind of poison it was, it must present with the same symptoms as asthma," I said then rattled off what they were. "Tightening of the chest. Shortness of breath. Coughing. He must've thought he was having an asthma attack, so he kept taking puffs."

"But for two days?"

"Maybe at first he was really having one. I don't know. He used his inhaler to help. But at some point, someone switched his for one that was filled with poison."

"Who?"

"Good question," I said. "Something we have to find out."

"I have to find out," Pogue said. "Me. Okay?"

"Okay." Not sure what I said to make him defensive.

"So. Two hundred people were there. And now there's no telling where they all are. Right?"

"I know," I said. "It's gonna make it really hard for you. Plus, it appears lots of people had access to his inhaler and some even carried a spare."

"What do you mean?"

I explained to him what I had learned.

"Romaine, you are going to have to help me."

"Help you how?" I asked. It seemed since I'd been back that had become the favorite phrase of Auntie Zanne and Pogue. But I didn't know what he meant, because from what I understood, he'd told me to butt out.

"You have to be the medical examiner."

"No, I don't."

"Yes you do."

"Why do I have to do that?" I'm sure my tone came off a little nastier than I intended. "I can't take a job I have no intention of keeping."

"And you don't have to take it permanently. But, if this is a murder, I've got to investigate."

"Yeah, I think we've just established it is murder. And you just told me that you can do it without me."

"Yes. I can. And I will. Investigate that is. That's not the problem."

"Then what is?"

"If you don't help me then guess who will be legally obligated to do an inquest?"

"Who?" I said, but no sooner than I let the words out of

mouth, then I remembered who. "That old Hoot Owl that's who, huh?" I said and chuckled. "Auntie Zanne."

In Texas, where my Auntie Zanne reigned supreme, a Justice of the Peace didn't need a law degree, or any degree for that matter, and could be voted in–elected by popular vote. And she was popular.

A resident of Texas since migrating with her parents from Louisiana in the forties, Suzanne Derbinay was a member of the board of directors for the Tri-County Chamber of Commerce, and ranking member in a host of ladies' auxiliaries and clubs, including the Red Hat Society, the founding member of the Roble Booster Club, and the Distinguished Ladies' Society of Voodoo Herbalists. And as the founder and proprietor of The Ball Funeral Home & Crematorium, where there was a natural, steady influx of clients and their families, along with an abundance of calendars and refrigerator magnets to boast her services, Babet Derbinay, was a household name.

She won the election in a landslide.

As part of her duties as the Justice of the Peace, or "JP" in political-*ese*, as Auntie explained to me, she oversaw minor civil and criminal matters, and as she tried to do on that fateful day, conduct marriage ceremonies among other things.

Those "other things," I soon learned included conducting inquests.

An "inquest" according to the Texas Code of Criminal Procedure meant an investigation into the cause and circumstances of a death and a determination as to whether the death was caused by an unlawful act. On top of that, she could lawfully go around and obtain evidence needed to initiate a criminal prosecution.

The only thing that could stop her was me. That was, if I were the medical examiner.

That same law that gave her power, limited her in counties which had one. While negotiating to help redesign the ME office, I'd learned a thing or two about the structure of Texas law as it concerned their doctors who determined whether the manner of death was natural, accident or homicide.

The State of Texas had no say over medical examiners, it was the County Commissioners Court, and the controlling statute required that counties with a population of more than a million folks had to have a medical examiner office, while counties with a population of less than a million could opt to have one. Sabine County, where Roble was located, Shelby County and San Augustine County combined, had little more than 45,000 residents, but the three counties had decided together to have their own ME office and had hired a medical examiner. Up until a month ago that had been Dr. Harley Westin—Doc Westin to everyone who knew him.

I thought about my feisty little auntie and how pushy and secretive she'd been during the last murder investigation. She had taken the murdered victim being discovered in her place of business as a personal assault to her reputation, and accused Pogue of having had a personal vendetta against Josephine Gail, wanting to frame her for the murder. She kept up the façade for nearly the entire investigation, and all the while contended that my poor Aunt Julep, Pogue's mother, was the culprit.

"What do you want me to do?" I asked.

"The autopsy," he said.

"Okay," I nodded although he couldn't see me. "I can do that."

"And nothing else, Romie."

"What does that mean?"

"I want to solve this case myself. Last time you convinced me to go away then you took over the entire investigation."

"I did not," I said defensively. "You'd signed up for that conference before I'd even come back to Roble."

"Yeah, you did. However it went, in the end it made me look incompetent."

"Incompetent to whom?" This was all in his head.

"Everybody."

I took in a breath. I didn't believe it, but evidently he did. "Okay," I said.

"What do we need to do now to get this started?" he said.

"I," I emphasized the word, "will need to call the hospital and have the body brought over to the new facility. I'll let the County Commissioners Court know."

"Can't we do like last time and I just appoint you?"

"You really didn't appoint me last time. I subbed for Doc Westin, he gave me permission to do it, not you."

"Oh. I thought I had been the one who gave the permission."

"No. But it's okay. I've met all the people in charge. I'm on good terms—very good terms with them."

"Okay, then you'll do like last time and give me the report."

"Yep."

He paused. I could hear him breathing hard. "You're not mad are you?" he asked.

"No, Cousin. Not at all."

I hung up from Pogue, opened up a browser window on my computer and pulled up my email. I clicked on old mail and found a recent correspondence with one of the Commissioners. I composed a quick email relaying my sense that there may have been foul play in Michael Hackett's death and, in my medical opinion, deemed it necessary to perform an autopsy. I also added, since I'd been so adamant about not working for the tri-county, that if I was not deemed suitable to do it, I strongly suggested that an ME from another county perform one before burial. I sent it and stared at the ad that popped up afterward.

"That's all I can do," I said to the screen. "And it appears that's all that Pogue wants me to do."

"You talking to your computer?" Auntie had come into my room and stood in the archway that separated the sitting room from the sleeping area.

"It's better than talking to the dead," I said.

"That's a matter of opinion," she said.

I didn't answer her. I stared at my monitor and thought about Bumper. He was so young. So much promise ahead of him. Why would someone want to take that away?

"I see you're lost in thought," Auntie said. "I just wanted to come and check on you, make sure you were alright."

She turned to walk away, but I called her name, stopping her. I thought maybe I should tell her my idea of what happened to Bumper. Pogue just wanted to keep it official. It would be nice to have someone to bounce around ideas with. "Can you keep a secret?" I asked.

"Oh heavens no!" She let her eyes roll upward. "As soon as you tell me all of Roble will know. Heck all of East Texas." She patted my head. "When it comes to you telling me secrets to keep, best thing for you to remember is mum's the word."

Chapter Thirteen

There were mums all over the kitchen table when I came down for breakfast the next day. Big. White. Fluffy.

"Homecoming," I muttered.

The silk chrysanthemum scattered about were used to make "mums" for girls and arm garters for boys, a tradition worn during homecoming for as long as anyone could remember. Mostly exclusive to Texas, the adornment was virtually unknown anywhere else. Sporting one, most Texans believed, began at Baylor University in Waco (others erroneously believe the tradition started in Missouri) and began with live mums worn as a corsage but morphed, like most things Texas, to something huge.

Now the mum flower was just the base and they were made with trailing ribbons and feather boas that when pinned, could cover half the chest and were long enough to reach the floor. Festooned with personalized trinkets of the kind seen on charm bracelets, popular with people of all ages, it had borne a lucrative industry with mum businesses popping up everywhere.

"I guess there's no bacon," I said. Josephine Gail and Auntie Zanne were sitting at the table, mums up to their elbows. The weekend before it had been wedding decorations I had to wade through. Catfish had warned me that homecoming was coming, I should have figured it was going to interfere somehow with me.

"Looks like you're going to have to go for a bowl of cereal on the back porch today," Auntie Zanne said. "Can't have all that bacon grease popping all over my mums."

"Why are you making them here?" I asked.

"We're not making them, we're dismantling them."

"You're dismantling them?" I asked. "Catfish said homecoming was this weekend."

"It is. But these are the ones we made for the wedding party to wear."

"Bumper and Jorianne had been homecoming king and queen during their senior year in high school," Josephine Gail said, "and they were going to be honored."

"Not you too, Josephine," I said. "I didn't know you were part of the booster club."

"I'm not. Just giving Babet a helping hand." She was all smiles, having come out of her last depression soon after we solved the first murder. I looked at her. Bad dye job on her probably gray, but now yellowish-colored hair. Her eyes bright, cheeks rosy, I hoped that the murder that was starting to brew in my mind, didn't give her flashbacks and send her over the edge again.

"I could use as many hands as I can get," Auntie Zanne said and patted the chair next to her.

"We're only about halfway finished," Josephine Gail said. "We've still got to make the new ones."

"You're making more?"

"Yes," Auntie said. "More somber. Less festive." She held up the one she was working on. "I had even thought of using black mums."

"Oh my goodness," I said. "That would be morbid."

"That's what I told her," Josephine Gail said. "I had to stop her from picking them up at Michael's when we went up to Houston."

"Why do you need to redo them, anyway?" I asked.

"The wedding party is still coming to Homecoming, only now we're doing a tribute to Bumper."

"Couldn't you just reorder the ones you need instead of trying to do this yourself?" I knew she must've used one of the many mum companies to get the ones she had for Homecoming.

"The JOY Club made them," Auntie said.

JOY, an acronym for, Just Older Youth, was a Tri-County's senior group. The club had a hand in most of the annual activities that happened. Manning booths, decorating, making phone calls. They had been in existence since I could remember, even before it was popular to show that people could still be active in their sixties and beyond.

"It was the first thing they'd done after Doc Westin died, and you know he was more than just a member, he was their doctor and leader," Auntie Zanne explained. "This homecoming was hard enough for them, because it was his favorite time of year. He loved football. I just didn't want them to know that we were taking apart all the work they'd put in while they were grieving, and what had been done in his honor."

"They really miss Doc Westin," Josephine Gail said. "Maybe you could see to them?"

"Me?"

"Not join the club," Josephine Gail said and chuckled. "I know you're not that old. But you could be their doctor seeing that you're taking over his practice."

My brow creased. "Doc Westin had a practice?"

"Not really," Auntie Zanne said. "He just cared for the members of the JOY Club, or if they sent someone to him. A lot of them couldn't afford all the doctoring they needed. He just supplemented."

"Oh," I said. "I didn't know that."

That must be what was in all those boxes, I thought. Doc Westin's patient files. I'd definitely have to go through them, I wasn't sure what he'd charted would be in any of their other patient files. Their other doctors should have all of their medical information.

"Lots of things around here you don't know about," Auntie Zanne. "But stick with me and I'll school you."

"Yeah," Josephine Gail said. "She knows a lot about a lot of things."

I saw Auntie squint her eyes and surreptitiously shake her

head as if she didn't want Josephine Gail to mention something.

"Oh!" Josephine Gail said. "You had two people stop by already this morning looking for you," she said. "Maybe you'll have a date for Homecoming."

"Who?"

"Catfish and Rhett," she said.

I rolled my eyes. "I don't think they were looking for me," I said. "Or wanting to take me to a high school dance."

"They asked about you. Didn't they, Babet?"

"They did, but you better watch it," Auntie said. "She's got a Yankee who's come a-courting. We don't want to start another war."

"Where is he? Your friend from Chicago," Josephine Gail asked. "I wanted to meet him."

"He's a busy man," Auntie said. "He's the Chief-of-Staff," she said. "I believe that might be his name as well."

"Okay," I said. "I'm just going to grab a bowl of cereal." It was healthier for me, plus I didn't want her to start on me about filling Doc Westin's footsteps, or about my Chief-of-Staff, or whether Catfish or Rhett were pining after me. And I certainly wasn't going to join the JOY Club or become any of their doctors.

"Romaine," Auntie Zanne said. She got up and walked to the stove. "I need you to ride with me over to Angel's Grace, there's something there I want to show you."

Grace Community Center, nicknamed Angel's Grace, was the county's outreach center—soup line, senior center, clothing drive headquarters and office of the Roble Belles, among other things.

"Are you going to tell her?" Josephine Gail said.

"Tell me what?" I asked.

"Don't go spilling the beans, Josephine Gail," Auntie said.

I looked at the two of them. They were up to something. Leave it to them to try to play matchmaker or something. I wasn't falling for it.

"I can't go," I said.

"Why?" Auntie Zanne said. "What do you have to do?" She

raised an eyebrow.

I had an autopsy to do, but I couldn't tell her that because Pogue didn't want anyone to know that it might just be murder. The Commissioners hadn't wasted any time getting back to me telling me to go ahead and proceed with it. They were happy to have me do it. But, if I mentioned to Auntie Zanne that I was doing one, she would keep poking until she figured out who or backed me into a corner and I confessed. For all intents and purposes, the new ME office was finished so I couldn't use that as an excuse, and Alex still hadn't made an appearance electronically or in the flesh.

"Do I have time to eat?" I was going to have to go along with what she wanted in order not to spill the beans, so I conceded. I didn't want to have to keep up with lies.

"Of course you do," she smiled sweetly. "Take as long as you want."

I knew that meant for me to hurry up. If I didn't, she'd start with her nagging.

"How about if I just grab a piece of fruit."

Chapter Fourteen

Mysteriously quiet all the way over to Angel's Grace, Auntie Zanne seemed lost in thought. Usually she was a chatterbox, trying to drag me into some activity she was doing. But not now. She sat calmly and stared out of the window. I didn't have any idea what she wanted with me. Probably wanting to wrangle me into some homecoming undertaking.

Whatever she had planned for me, the anticipation of it couldn't settle the butterflies I had for the secret I was hiding. I couldn't wait to start on that autopsy, especially in the brand spanking new facility. I kept checking the clock on the dashboard estimating the amount of time it would take me to help Auntie Zanne with whatever she needed, drop her back off at home and get over to the ME facility. The reason for an autopsy is a sad thing, sure enough, but actually performing one was exciting and exhilarating—at least to me. I really was a detective, searching for clues, putting them all together and making the ultimate decision that everyone else had to rely on.

And then the new facility itself. Even though I figured I'd never work there, I had suggested all the things I had wanted to work with, and lo and behold, they agreed to purchase them. Now, at the request of the sheriff, I was going to get to use them.

We arrived at the darkened and deserted building of Angel's Grace Community Center and Auntie Zanne led me to a room near the back door. Turning on only one or two lights as we passed, making it difficult to see as we walked through the rooms and down a long hallway to the rear of the building. She turned to look around several times, seemingly making sure no one was watching us, then once again as we stood in front of a door. She pulled out a key and opened up what looked like a storage closet.

"This is what I wanted you to see." She flicked the switch on the wall, illuminating the small space.

There were brooms, mops, shelves with paper products and in the middle were cases of a blue drink in clear bottles with black tops stacked two deep along the wall. Black wide-font letters printed across the front read: *Mighty Max.*

"What is this?" I asked.

"Mighty Max," she said.

I huffed. "I can see that."

"Then why did you ask me?"

"Why are you showing it to me?"

"I think it was the reason Bumper was murdered."

"What?" My mouth dropped open, and I felt my stomach lurch. "Did you say murdered?"

"You got cotton in your ears, Sugarplum?"

I couldn't believe she'd come to the same conclusion that I had, and she did it without saying one word to me about it. "What makes you think he was murdered?" I asked.

"Asthma is not contagious."

"What does that mean?"

"Whatever caused Bumper's death, made your Chief-of-Staff sick. Came back to pick you up looking like death warmed over. Cause of death couldn't have been asthma."

"Poison isn't contagious either," I said, intrigued at her reasoning.

"Don't play dumb with me, darlin'. It might not be contagious but a person can pick up poison from somewhere else, skin contact, ingestion. Don't you know that?"

"I do," I said, enjoying her line of reasoning.

"I think that's just what happened."

I smiled at her. I always fussed about her nosiness and

intrusive nature, but I felt the same way and was itching to look into it. but Pogue was locking me out. It was good to have someone to discuss it with.

"I think so too," I said.

She blew out a breath and then smiled back. "Good. I thought I was going to have to use up all my energy trying to convince you and I wouldn't have any left to get you to help me."

"Help you do what?"

"Solve it."

I chuckled. "You may not believe this is me talking, Auntie, but I am right with you."

"You are?"

"I am. That's exactly what I want to do."

She smacked her hands together. "Hot dog!" She shut the door to the closet and locked it. "C'mon," she said and grabbed hold of my arm. "Let me tell you what I think and you can help me plan the inquest."

Uh-oh.

That's just what Pogue said would happen. That big ole grin she was sporting was soon to disappear. I hated to do it to her, but I had to tell her she wasn't going to be the one to get the information to start the criminal investigation.

I waited until she sat down, then I sat opposite her and leaned in. "You're not going to do the inquest, Auntie."

"What are you talking about?" she said. "I'm the Justice of the Peace and we don't have an ME. It's in my job description."

"You don't have a *permanent* ME."

"What does that mean?"

"Pogue asked me to do the autopsy."

"He... You... How did... You're not even... Oh my gosh!" Her little face was turning red as half sentences sputtered out. She wasn't even able to complete a full thought.

"Spit it out, Auntie before you have some sort of stroke."

She stood up and kicked her foot. "How are you doing the autopsy? You're not the ME. I am duly elected to do the job when there's no ME."

"He didn't want you messing in his investigation."

"That little buster!" she said.

"You can be a bit... overbearing," I said, flinching at the same time, not wanting her to set her wrath on me.

"I knew you'd take his side."

"I'm not," I said. "He doesn't want me meddling in his investigation either. Said this time he wanted to solve this one himself. All on his own."

"That boy is all day stupid."

"All day stupid," I said at the same time she uttered the words. It was her go to phrase about Pogue.

"Well, if you're not helping who is doing the autopsy?"

"I told you, I am. But that's all he wants from me."

She stared at me for a moment, then a sly smile crossed her face. "But that's not all you're going to do, right?"

"I don't know, Auntie," I said, a mischievous look sprouting on my face to match hers. "I think I'm feeling just how you must feel when you're up to something you shouldn't be. I just want to poke my nose in it. I didn't realize it at the time, but as I look back I had such a good time solving that last murder."

"Me too," she said and clapped her hands. She pulled the chair to face me and plopped down. "We can do it together."

I tilted my head to the side. "I'd like that."

"Good," she said. "I know just where to start."

Chapter Fifteen

Auntie dragged me back to her secreted closet, pulled me inside and shut the door behind us. She flicked on the light.

"I think Bumper was killed as part of an FBI sting operation."

I closed my eyes and tried hard not to chuckle. Maybe I'd spoken too soon about joining forces with her. I should have known she was going to go all motion picture big on me.

"An FBI sting in Roble?" I asked, disbelief dripping in each word uttered.

"You don't believe me?"

"Is it that obvious?" I said.

"Are we working together on this or not?"

"That isn't exactly what I thought might've happened."

"See, that's how you collaborate on things like this. You'll get to say what you think happened, I tell you what I think. We compare notes and get this thing solved before Pogue."

"Not a race," I said, "and we can't get in his way."

"Deal," she said, more easily than I would have bet on.

"So tell me," I said, bracing myself so as not to keel over on hearing this hailstorm of a story she had evidently conjured up. "Why is it you think he was killed? Was it because of an FBI sting?"

"Don't patronize me," she said. She pointed her finger and narrowed her eyes. She could tell I was on the brink of breaking out into laughter "I have evidence of my conclusions."

I held up my hands in surrender. "Okay," I said. "I'm listening."

She reached between a row of cases, and pulled a newspaper that had been tucked behind them. "This is why," she said, and handed it to me.

I read the headline of the article she pointed to out loud. "Bribery and Kickbacks: The FBI's Basketball Sting." I looked at her. "I don't get it," I said.

"If you read the article, you'll see that financial advisors and tennis shoe companies are paying kickbacks to assistant coaches who get players to go to certain schools or do business with them after they make the NBA."

I let my eyes scan the article. Several assistant basketball coaches from Division I schools across the country had been arrested for taking money for recruiting high school players and steering them to certain colleges. Along with the coaches, a shoe manufacturing marketing exec and several financial advisors had been indicted. In addition, the article relayed, the targeted players and their parents were getting money as incentives to sign.

"This is about basketball," I said and handed her back the newspaper.

"I know," she said and frowned. "I read it."

"What does it have to do with Bumper?" Trying to get information from her in one cohesive stream, whether she wanted to share it or not, was like pulling teeth. "Am I supposed to guess?"

"No. I'll tell you." She put the newspaper back in its hiding place and picked up one of the bottles of green liquid. "This is a sports drink that uses NFL players for endorsements." She handed me the bottle. "And Texas A&M is a Mighty Max endorsed school."

"Okay." I rolled the bottle around in my hand. I wouldn't ever drink anything green, but according to the label it was an organic sports drink packed with electrolytes.

"There's probably other schools, but that's the only one I know about right now." She gave me a nod that said she was going to find out more. "Then there's this Coach Harold 'Buddy' Budson." She did the air quotes thing. "He's one of the assistant coaches over there."

"At A&M?"

"Yes," she said. "And he and this Mighty Max marketing guy -"

"What's his name?"

"Shane Blanchard."

"Okay."

"The two of them were trying to recruit Bumper. I mean really hard. They came down to go to almost every home game, went and had meetings and dinners over at his house, met his parents, the whole nine yards."

"But isn't that what they're supposed to do? Coaches, recruiters or whomever when they're recruiting—meet the parents, share what they have to offer?"

"Yes, but just like Piper said, they're not supposed to offer money."

"Did they offer Bumper money?"

"That's what I think happened. They offered him money to get him to go to Texas A&M."

"And he turned them down," I said finishing her little scenario. "So they killed him."

"Yes."

"That was a couple years ago. Mrs. Hackett said Bumper was a junior. They're not even here."

"They are so here. Came down here on the pretense of watching this year's football players."

"On the pretense?"

"Yes. A recruiting mission."

I chuckled. "Yeah. Again that's what they do. Don't they come every year?"

"Of course they do. They don't try to keep me off their trail by trying to bribe me with cases of their hormone-filled blue water."

"I don't know, Auntie. That's pretty far-fetched," I said. "Only thing we know for sure is that he didn't pick Texas A&M two or three years ago. You don't even know if they offered him money, or that perhaps USC offered him more money."

"Michael Hackett, Sr. drives a Saturn. They don't even make

those cars anymore. Bumper didn't take any money to play ball."

"Auntie, this is just so out there." I shook my head. "It would take me some time to wrap my head around this. And," I looked around the closet and placed my hand on the doorknob, "be outside the confines of this small space. Can we talk about this outside of this claustrophobia-inducing cubby?"

"I have to tell you one more thing."

"Okay," I said.

She looked around, as if someone might have just snuck inside the closet to spy on us, then she leaned in, licked her lips and whispered. "I think FBI agent, Rhett Remmiere, on an undercover assignment, is in charge of the whole sting operation."

Chapter Sixteen

"Oh brother!" I said. It was too much for me to try and control my reaction to her machinations. I had to laugh.

Rhett Remmiere had apparently just shown up one day on Auntie Zanne's door step. According to her, he was not only FBI, but a certified spy. He, when I confronted him about his credentials, wouldn't ever say for sure. Although he did deny being "certified" verifying that there wasn't any such thing.

Now Auntie had the man in charge of a newsworthy, multi-university sting operation. The only thing I knew he did was drive a hearse.

"Don't be so surprised," she said as I laughed. "It happens all the time."

"And you know all about that, huh?"

"Of course I do. Everyone does. You know it's like in that movie *The Godfather*," Auntie said following me out of her closet, shutting off the light and locking the door behind her.

"I don't think there were FBI agents in *The Godfather*."

"Sure, the one agent went undercover and got so involved in it that he became one of them."

"I think what you're thinking of the movie *Donnie Briscoe*," I said.

"Yeah," she said, agreeing with me although I was telling her she was wrong. "That's the one. Don or Donnie if that's what you want to call him, was the one that was the godfather."

"If Rhett's undercover, why is he using his real name?" I

wasn't going to try to explain to her that *Donnie* was the guy's name and not his title.

"Maybe he isn't," she said. "You ever thought of that?"

"No," I said.

"And why did he come to Roble and get a job?" she asked. "He's from Houston, who'd want to come here?"

"That's what I'm always telling you," I said. "Why leave Chicago to come back here. And if he is in charge, then he either thinks you're involved or he's been using you all the time."

"Oh phooey, he is not using me. If he needed me as part of the sting, he could have just asked me." She waved a hand at me. "And," she drew the word out, "I'm not talking about you coming to a small town," she said. "This is your home. Only family you have left is here. You should want to be here. But not Rhett. He has no reason. Unless..." She wiggled her eyebrows.

"So that's what you think Rhett is doing here," I said. "He's working at your funeral home because he is on an undercover assignment to weed out college football coaches involved in a bribery and gratuity scheme."

"Exactly!" she said.

"I was being sarcastic," I said.

"But you hit the nail right on the head. It's exactly what I think is going on."

"So in your madcap scheme of federal proportions, who is the killer?"

"Have you been listening to me?" she asked.

"Unfortunately," I said, "I heard every word."

"Then you should know."

This time I was sure she was going to make me guess.

"Uh. Let me think." I tilted my head and rested my eyes on a spot on the ceiling. "In your newspaper article it was the coaches and marketing guy." I looked at her. "There's been no financial advisors around here, right?"

"No."

"Okay. Then my guess is Coach Buddy and Shane Bouchard."

"Blanchard. His name is Shane Blanchard."

"Oh yeah, Blanchard." I nodded. "That's who I think." I looked at her. "Did I guess right?"

"You did," she said. "But there's another one to add."

"Who?"

"Shhh! Did you hear that?" Auntie stood up and walked over to the entryway to the adjoining room.

"I didn't hear anything," I said. "And why do you think someone would be listening in anyway? You've been jumpy ever since we got here."

"What we're talking about is high op kind of stuff."

I laughed.

"Don't laugh," she said, giving me a cautious look. "The ones that killed Bumper could kill us the same way."

"And how did they kill him?" I asked.

"I don't know," she said, her eyes darting around in the dimly lit space. "I was waiting until I did my inquest to find out. I just knew until then I had to be careful of what I ate and drank. That's why I've got that closet locked."

"Don't tell me you think that they poisoned their sports drink. That would be a media nightmare for them."

"I'm still working out the kinks in all of this. That's what I do as justice of the peace, you know?"

"And you know, even with you being 'duly elected', you still couldn't have performed an autopsy."

"I was meaning to read up on the rules about that."

I laughed. "All the reading in the world won't get you qualified to do that."

Chapter Seventeen

I was finally on my way to perform the autopsy. It was going to be the first one in the new facility. I'd invited Auntie to go with me, she was happy to leave Angel's Grace and whoever's prying eyes and ears she felt were there. She was elated to be a part of the first leg of the investigation with me. You'd have thought she'd won the Publishing House Sweepstakes.

Before we left Angel's Grace for the ME's office, I called the hospital and spoke to a person in the morgue at Sabine County Hospital to arrange to have Michael "Bumper" Hackett's body brought over.

On this leg of the trip, Auntie was Chatty Cathy. She was just as excited as I was.

"Remember," she said. "We have to talk to him."

"You remember," I said. "I don't talk to dead people. That's what you do."

"But it'll help us figure out what he died from."

"That's the purpose of the autopsy, Auntie. Science giving us the answers because the decedent can't tell us."

"Oh hogwash. There are spirits everywhere. And the dead person's spirit keeps close to his body."

"That's the difference in me and you," I said.

"What?" she said. "You don't believe that spirits can give us answers."

"I believe we'll solve this from the clues we'll glean along the way. Scientific evidence will not only lead us to the killer, but will convict him. Or her."

"And who do you think the evidence is going to lead you to?" she asked.

"Well, I've been thinking," I said. "I came up with three people who in my mind are persons of interests."

"There you go using Pogue's term. Isn't that what he called his suspects on the last murder we solved? Persons of interest?" She shook her head. "Just call them what they are, suspects."

"Okay," I said. "These are the people that made it to my suspect list," I glanced over at her. "Ready?"

"Shoot."

"Okay. Bonnie Alvarez. Piper Alvarez. And the best man. I haven't found out his name yet."

"Chase Turner," Auntie said. "I had to know it for the program."

"Chase Turner," I murmured, committing his name to memory. "Do you know him? Did he play football with Bumper?"

"No, he didn't play ball for Roble. He was older than Bumper. I'd seen him around before, but he left and went to the military."

"Oh," I said.

"Why those three?" Auntie asked.

"Because they all disappeared at the wedding, which gave them the opportunity to poison him. I never saw Bonnie Alvarez before or after the incident. I wouldn't have known she was there except Mr. Alvarez said she was."

"You said Bonnie had a 'shotgun' pointing at Bumper and that was the reason he was getting married," Auntie said. "If she wanted him to marry her daughter why would she kill him?"

"I also said Bumper was marrying Jorianne because she was pregnant. But I've changed my mind."

"I heard Bonnie and Piper talking in the room while we were waiting on the ambulance where the girls were getting changed," Auntie Zanne said. "I'd gone in to get the guns."

"You heard them?"

"Yes, I did. And they sounded pretty suspicious to me."

"What did they say?"

"Bonnie and Piper agreed this marriage wasn't good for Jorianne. That she was rushing into things, and she needed to learn to be more independent."

"That's what Piper said when she was at the Hacketts' place."

"I know," Auntie said. "That's why I asked about the caterer. I thought since they hired the caterer, they might have been able to get him, unwittingly, to serve Bumper something that was poisonous."

I looked over at her. "You suspected it was foul play when we were at the Hacketts?"

"I suspected it as soon as I saw your Chief-of-Staff's lips."

"Can we just call him Alex? Please."

Auntie laughed. "Okay, we can. I just thought you liked to call him that. So," she turned to me, "when did you first suspect it was murder?"

"It wasn't then," I said. "Not that soon. But after we got back from seeing Mrs. Hackett, I started thinking about it."

"Something how we thought the same thing."

"Yes, it is." I took my eyes off the road momentarily to smile at her. "So, did your questions about the caterer help your case any?"

"It does in a way." Auntie rubbed her fingers across her temple. "If they're all are in cahoots—"

"Who?" I asked, interrupting.

"The A&M coach and the Mighty Max guy, then it makes sense that they wanted to shut Bumper up."

"How does that make sense?"

"He turned A&M down sure enough, but what if there's an FBI sting operation taking place, he would've been the star witness."

"So they wanted to eliminate anyone who could testify against them?"

"That's what I'm thinking."

"I guess that could be right if it were true that they offered Bumper money."

"That Shane Blanchard asked me about setting up a

scholarship to be given each year to outstanding football players who are juniors."

"A scholarship is not a bribe. It has to be earned," I said.

"It could be a front. And it could be them trying to get me on their side so I won't be suspicious. Like giving me cases of that blue slime."

"I don't know," I said. "That doesn't make me think anything out of the ordinary."

"Does this make you think anything out of the ordinary?" she said, and moved closer to me. "He told me that he wanted me to be their 'supporter.' He said as the lead booster member I could play a part in his recruitment efforts."

"Shane Blanchard said that?"

"Yep. Sure did."

"That sounds a little suspicious, I guess."

"See," she said and nodded.

"Did he tell you how you were supposed to help?"

"Not yet. But now that he's on our radar we can get him to talk."

"He's not on my radar," I said.

"Why not?" she asked.

"Do you think anyone was actually offered money?"

"LaJay Reid goes to Texas A&M," she said and raised an eyebrow.

"He does?"

"He does. That's the other person I'm thinking is wrapped up in this thing," she said. "And, up until a week before he committed, everyone thought he was going to Arizona."

"Did he get money?"

"He got a new car for graduation. A big, shiny new truck."

"So maybe you should put him on your list," I said and glanced over at her. "He sure did have the opportunity to do it."

"He is on my list. I just told you he is the other person I was trying to tell you about when we were at the community center," she said. "And, in case you haven't noticed, he's got a thing for

Jorianne."

"I did notice him seeing to her when we were waiting on the ambulance," I said. "But I didn't think it was strange. He and Bumper were best friends, only natural he'd see to her."

"If they were best friends, why wasn't he Bumper's best man?"

"Ahh, good question," I said, nodding. "Why wasn't he indeed?"

Chapter Eighteen

"Hello, Bumper," Auntie walked to the front doors with me when the ambulance arrived with the body. She laid her hand on him and spoke to him through his black bag as they wheeled the gurney into the autopsy room. "We're here to see what happened to you. To take care of everything."

The attendant looked at me as I signed the release form attached to his clipboard. "She talks to dead people," I said and smiled.

He chuckled. "Do they ever talk back?" he asked.

"She says they do," I said then leaned in close. "They let her out of the home for the day and we forgot to bring her medication."

He laughed as he took the signed form and left.

As I unzipped Bumper from his ebony-colored cocoon, Auntie's conversation went into full swing. She pulled up a metal stool, sat at his head and chatted away. She told him all about her having people check their guns at the door, and how much trouble people gave her when it was time to give them back. How no one ever got to taste the food, and if that might have been a good thing seeing where he ended up. Then, she told him how pretty Jorianne looked and how she wished he could have seen her.

I pulled out the digital camera and started taking pictures.

"What a silly thing for the groom not to be able to see the bride in her wedding dress," she continued, "what about if he died, like you did before the ceremony? How would he ever know how beautiful she looked?"

"Is this what you usually say to your dead guests?" I interjected, pausing my picture taking to query her.

"No," she said, thoughtfully. "I usually talk about their family. Like who cried the most during our initial meeting, who was the phoniest, who was willing to fork over money if the insurance didn't cover the burial. People want to know how their love ones reacted to their deaths."

"Do they now," I said, trying not to laugh.

"Yes really," she said. "But this is my first autopsy so I just thought I'd talk about a range of things and see what sticks."

"With all your talking, it feels like the only thing sticking is a dagger in my side. You're killing me and if you don't pipe down," I said, "it'll be your last autopsy." I snapped a picture of her. "At least with me."

She held up her hand to shield her face.

"Don't take my picture. Did you see that, Bumper? She doesn't take this seriously, does she?"

I let her talk while I finished taking photos, putting my gear on and stuffing her into a safety shield and gown, but when I pulled down the mic close to me to start the autopsy, I had to shush her.

"Auntie," I said, "I can't have my dictation peppered with your ramblings. Time to stop that inane chatter."

"I'm just making him comfortable so he'll tell us all he knows. I told him we need his help to find out who did this to him."

"I heard you. Are you finished, yet?" I asked.

"Yes. I think so," she said, sincerity in her voice. "Just one more thing I need to say."

"What?" I asked.

"No. I mean to Bumper."

"Oh. Well, go ahead."

"I just want to apologize, Bumper. I'm so very sorry this happened to you. Especially that it happened to you at my place."

"Is that it?"

"Yep," she said, and gave a single nod.

I turned on the mic, and then she leaned in close to Bumper

and I heard her whisper, "She's so snippy."

"I heard that," I said. "And so did my mic. I need to do the talking now. Me into my mic." I pointed up to it. "It's time to open him up and get down to business."

"Okay," she said and hopped off the stool. "You take care of your business, while I take care of mine. I have to run to the little girl's room. By the time I get back, you'll probably be inside and we can see what really happened to poor little Bumper."

"Fine," I said, letting my voice get louder as she moved farther away from me. "Just no more talking once you get back."

I took the scalpel in hand and ran my hand over his chest. I cleared my throat and spoke loudly into the mic. "Male. Caucasian. Six feet, three inches tall. Two hundred twenty pounds. All tattoos, scars and identifying marks will be documented photographically."

I bent over the body ready to make my thoracoabdominal Y-shaped incision, but before I did, I turned to make sure Auntie wasn't in earshot, then turned back and looked at the young football player and almost husband and father. "Okay, Bumper Hackett," I said. "If you *can* talk, now's the time."

Chapter Nineteen

During the autopsy, Bumper didn't say one word, and, to my surprise, neither did my zany auntie. She later told me she was so fascinated and proud to watch me work that she'd been flabbergasted.

"Well what did you learn?" she asked as we stood at the sink and washed our hands. She hadn't done anything to dirty hers, but she was enjoying the moment. "Was he murdered?"

"I think so," I said and nodded. I dried my hands as I walked over to the desk and sat down, she trailed behind me. "I don't like to give anything definite until I get a toxicology report in my hands." I threw the paper towel into the trash. Picking up the sheet of paper that I needed to fill out to have the samples taken to the lab, I waved it at her.

"How long will that take?" she said, sitting in the chair across from me, she pointed at the paper.

"That's according to what it is, but probably not more than a couple of days." I started checking off boxes, a rote activity for me. "I'll scan this request and then email it in. They'll have them tonight, then we'll get the results whenever they get to it."

"We don't have to wait until then to start investigating, do we?"

"No. We can go with what we know now."

"Which is?"

I looked up from my paperwork, tapping the pen on the desk. "Well..." I thought about her question. "I don't think it was a fast-acting poison," I said.

"Why?"

"Because of my observations of him on the day he died, and because of the pulmonary edema I found," I said. "Plus, we know that Bumper didn't take anything while he was at the house."

"Nothing other than his inhaler," she said.

"That's what I think killed him."

"What?" she asked. "You do?"

"Yep. I think it was poison in the inhaler."

"You didn't tell me that."

"I'm telling you now."

"Are you going to test the inhaler?"

"I don't have it."

"Where is it?"

"That's a good question, Auntie," I said. "I don't know where it is. Do you know what happened to it?"

"No." She shook her head thoughtfully. "I don't know anything about it," she said.

"Someone must have picked it up," I said.

"Maybe that's the someone who put the poison in it." She raised an eyebrow.

"Maybe," I said. "We need to try and figure out what happened to it."

Auntie shrugged. "We'll ask."

"Who?"

"Everyone who was around him, up in that gazebo."

"That'll work," I said.

"So someone put a slow-acting poison into that inhaler he had?" Auntie said.

"Or even in several inhalers. There were so many floating around, and that way they could be sure he got the poison inside of him."

"Is that possible?" she asked, looking at me. "For it to be several of them? Wouldn't that mean it was more than one person who killed him? That people were acting in concert with each other?"

"I don't know."

"Well, that would match my theory," she said. "Coach Buddy and Shane Blanchard is who I think did it. And maybe even LaJay was involved with them."

"I don't know that they had access to Bumper's inhalers, though," I said. "They weren't even at the wedding."

"LaJay had access, and he was at the wedding," Auntie said. "They could have planned it together and assigned him to be the one to carry it out."

"I thought you liked him," I said, and scrunched up my eyes. She could turncoat on a friend in five seconds flat. "You were nice to him when we went to see Mrs. Hackett."

"I like him fine. He's a good football player. But he's still a scoundrel."

I chuckled. "How so?"

"Going after your friend's girl is how. I told you he did that, remember. I heard even some say that he might be the father of Jorianne's baby, and that's why she was in such a rush to marry Bumper."

"I don't know about that," I said, and sucked my tongue. "That would be hard to hide. LaJay is black. Bumper and Jorianne are not. The baby would tell the story as soon as it arrived."

"I'm just telling you what I heard."

"Rumors are just that for the most part, Auntie. Can't rely on them."

"Maybe not, but they give you something to go on. It helped me to form my opinion about who might have killed Bumper."

"But we're going to follow the facts," I said. "We're not going to pick a person who you think did it and try to make the facts fit them."

"I wouldn't do that," she said. She pursed her lips and frowned, her feelings evidently hurt.

"That's what you did on the last murder we tried to solve." Her sad face wasn't going to alter the truth of the matter.

"We didn't *try* to solve it," Auntie said. "We did solve it."

"That we did." I smiled at her. "Still we are going to go about this the right way."

"Okay, so what do we do?"

"First things first," I said. "I have to finish up here—get the labs sent off and type up a report for Pogue."

"Don't tell him what we found out," Auntie said.

"I have to," I said. "Remember we're playing fair. And anything significant we find out we share."

"I'm not telling him about my theory," she said.

"That's okay," I said. "Because your theory is waaay out there. I think he'd appreciate me not telling him about that."

And, I thought, *he'd have a conniption if he knew Auntie had a hand in any of this.*

"You finish the report, then what?"

"Then I think we need to figure out where the inhalers came from, and where the inhaler he had when he collapsed went to."

"I don't know about the one he had, but didn't Delores say she had had the ones that got passed out?" Auntie said.

"Some of them, but I thought she said some of them were new."

Auntie shrugged.

"Either way," I said. "We need to know. Do you know where she would have gotten them from? Who Bumper's doctor was?"

"No," she said, and shook her head. "But McDougal is the only pharmacy in town. She would have probably gone there. Plus, he gives the football team a discount."

"Giving gratuities to the football players seems like a common occurrence around here," I said. "The pharmacy. The caterer. I don't understand how you figured those same actions precipitated a murder."

"It's different when outsiders are involved. Those men—Shane and Coach Buddy are from big universities, and even bigger cities. Criminal behavior is stitched into their fiber."

"That's not a nice thing to say," I said.

"May not be nice," she said, "but in this case, I think it might be true."

"And what if it's not? What if they didn't do it? After you've talked about these people, practically defaming them. Damage done. Then what?"

"Well, darlin', then I'll just apologize." She smiled. "Now come on, I'll be up all night embalming Bumper if we don't get a move on. I'll have to call Rhett to bring the hearse over. My good, sweet friend, Delores Hackett, is counting on me, and I can't let her down."

"Okay." I flipped over page the I was working on and signed the request, finishing up all I needed to do for the lab. Then I shuffled through the papers to find the release form I needed to give to the funeral home. I read the name and address of who'd be picking up the body and I cringed. That's when I realized that my ride home was going to be awful.

I put down my pen. "Auntie," I said and took in a breath. "I have something to tell you."

Chapter Twenty

"That woman is as loyal as Benedict Arnold!"

It was the next morning after she'd gotten the news and Auntie Zanne was still upset that Delores Hackett had gone with another funeral home to handle the remains of her only child.

We'd planned to go to McDougal's Pharmacy first thing, but I didn't know if I could take another car ride with her. She had fussed all the way home the night before, and it looked as if she still wasn't going to let the perceived slight go even though it was a brand new day. I just knew if I rode in the car with her, having to endure another round of kicking and screaming, I was going to have to prescribe myself a sedative.

Auntie Zanne was sitting at the kitchen table when I came down, three pots boiling on the stove filled with who knows what each with as much steam coming out of it as she had coming out of her.

"How dare her not entrust her son's remains to Ball Funeral Home."

"Maybe it was because it had bad memories for her," I said. "This is where..." I rocked my head from side to side. "You know... Where it happened."

"Oh just spit it out. Where Bumper was murdered. You don't have to be discreet when it's me you're talking to."

Pogue had had to let Mrs. Hackett know the reason I was doing the autopsy, and I thought, and thoroughly understood how that could have played a part in her not choosing Auntie's place.

She hadn't had any say over what happened with her son once I made my determination because state law requires that if an ME or justice of the peace deemed one necessary, the family couldn't fight it.

It must have been hard for her to lose her son at our house, and me being the one to determine he'd been murdered.

"Auntie, maybe you should just have a cup of tea," I suggested.

"Don't tell me what to do," she grumbled.

"I'm not, but you have to be in a better frame of mind when we go to the pharmacy."

"There is nothing wrong with my frame of mind."

"Do you want me to just go by myself?" I asked. "I can share notes when I get home."

"Oh you want to snub me, too?"

"Oh, geesh." I shook my head. "No. I don't want to snub you. And I don't think Mrs. Hackett did either."

"How about if we just go?" she said.

I didn't have much choice but to agree with that. She wasn't going to let me go by myself, and she wasn't going to get over not being given the care of Bumper.

"I'm driving," she said and snatched the keys off the wall caddy.

That made me so nervous that I started to run upstairs and grab my St. Christopher medallion.

"So what's our plan?" Auntie glanced over at me from behind the steering wheel. I'd made sure my seatbelt was tight and I braced my hand against the dashboard. We'd driven half way there in silence. I had kept a watchful eye wondering if I was going to see steam rising from her too-high hairdo. Her words now, though, were even and much calmer than they had been before we left the house.

I shrugged. "We ask him questions. Primarily, I guess, if he knew who wrote the script for Bumper's inhalers." I shook my head. "I hope that he won't give us a problem about sharing the information without Pogue around."

"We don't need Pogue, Sugarplum." She smiled for the first time. "I'm the justice of the peace, I can initiate an investigation."

"Auntie, I'm aware of what you can do, but you having that power is scary."

She produced a wide grin that showed all of her teeth.

"Hi Babet," Mr. McDougal said as we walked in the door, the bell overhead jingling our arrival. He'd been the town's pharmacist probably for the last thirty or more years.

"Morning," she said. "How are you this fine morning?"

"I can't complain," he said. "And don't tell me this is Romaine? I haven't seen her in years."

I usually came into town, visited my family and got out before anyone in town could see me. And I had planned to keep a low profile while I waited my time out this time. But with the murders that kept popping up, I might not be as low key as I'd planned.

"Oh. My. Lord. Will you look at this!" Auntie said. She grabbed a newspaper from the stand in front of the pharmacy counter, completely ignoring Mr. McDougal's comment. She threw the paper on the counter and planted her hands on her hips.

"What is it?" I said picking up the paper.

"Can't you read?" Auntie voice had gone up several octaves and decibels. "I swear! Are they trying to put me out of business?"

The headline read: "Another Murder at a Roble Funeral Home."

"Oh wow," I said.

"Wow doesn't cover it," she said. "Who in the world is writing this stuff?"

"Shame what happened over at your place," Mr. McDougal said, his expression not changing. "When I first heard about it, they were sure he'd pull through because it had been only been an asthma attack. Too bad, he was one of those really nice boys, was going to make something of himself."

"Well, it wasn't asthma that done him in," Auntie huffed.

"Hi, Mr. McDougal," I said interrupting her before she shared information best kept secret for the time being. "Good to see you."

I knew to be polite to him, not just because I was brimming with questions, but because it was how I was raised. Auntie Zanne was giving me enough grief, without me "causing her embarrassment by not minding my manners." Although, her attitude so far that morning hadn't been exemplary.

"How is everything with you?" he asked. "And with Chicago?"

"She's back to stay," Auntie stopped huffing long enough to disseminate some misinformation. "She's taking Doc Westin's place as the ME."

I frowned and opened my mouth to correct what she'd said. Why she continued to tell people things about me that weren't true, I just couldn't understand. But I didn't want to make a scene and call her out in front of a man we needed. I wanted him to see that we were on the same accord.

"We wanted to ask you some questions," I said and nudged Auntie Zanne to the back of me. "About Michael Hackett's asthma."

"She means Bumper. No need to be formal, right, McDougal?" Auntie Zanne said, stepping back up next to me. "We want to know what went wrong with his inhaler."

"Wrong with it? I don't know of anything that can go wrong with an inhaler. It's not a mechanical instrument."

"It didn't work," Auntie said.

"The only reason I'd know that it wouldn't work would be that it was empty or outdated."

"I don't think that happened either," she said.

"You think someone tampered with them?" he asked.

"We don't know," I said, "because we don't have the inhaler he used to look at." Auntie Zanne just couldn't control herself. I was going to have to speak with her about how to conduct an investigation.

"Who prescribed the inhalers for him?" I asked.

"And remember," Auntie Zanne said, "I'm the Justice of the Peace. I'm sworn by law to find out what happened, and you have to uphold it by cooperating."

"I voted for you, Babet," he said smiling. "And I have every intention on being helpful. I just think it's awful what happened."

"Well, thank you for your vote. I will make sure I live up to the confidence you have in me."

"Uh. Back to the inhalers," I said and again side-stepped Auntie. "Can you look up the name of the doctor who prescribed the inhaler for him?"

"Of course, I can, but I don't need to. When he was younger it was his pediatrician, Dr. Granger over in San Augustine, but during his last few years in high school it was Doc Westin."

"Doc Westin?" I said, surprised. "Are you sure?"

"One hundred percent. But still I hadn't seen one of those prescriptions since Bumper left for college."

"That was two years ago," Auntie said. She looked at me. "Were all of them from back then?"

"I don't know," I said. "Would his mother give him something that old? It's no wonder they didn't work."

"They didn't have to work," Auntie Zanne, "they just needed to hold the poison."

"Poison! What kind of poison?" Mr. McDougal said. "It didn't say that in the paper, only that cause was undetermined, but not natural."

"Is that what you put on your paperwork?" Auntie said and looked up at me. "Undetermined?"

"I have to wait until the toxicology report comes back to make a definite determination."

"Can you imagine? Another murder in Roble," Mr. McDougal said. "And both of them at your place."

"They weren't both at my place," Auntie said. I knew she was going to get indignant.

"Let's go, Auntie," I said and tugged on her arm. "Thank you, Mr. McDougal." I waved bye as I pulled Auntie out of the door.

"So all we've discovered," Auntie said fastening her seat belt after we got back into the car, "is that Delores used a bunch of old inhalers to care for her son's asthma, and someone took one of those and filled it with poison."

"I wish we had that inhaler. Then we'd know exactly what poison was used and that might just help us narrow down who it could be."

"Well, we're going to look for it," Auntie Zanne said. "Plus, I thought you were sending a toxicology request."

"I did, although there are some poisons you have to specifically ask to be tested. I checked all the boxes, but I don't know what we'll get seeing this is such a small place."

"We are just as good as those labs up in Chicago," Auntie said.

"I'm not saying you're not," I said, then shook my head. "I only wish I had it, that's all."

"Well, I've been thinking about this, and with us needing that information, it might just be a good idea."

"What?" I asked.

"We have to go the funeral," Auntie Zanne said.

"I don't think that's a good idea."

"Why?"

"Because you can't go starting trouble at a person's funeral because they didn't pick you to do it."

"That's not why I think we should go."

"Okay. What's your reason then?"

"Because the killer might be there. And we can ask around and see what happened to that inhaler that Bumper had."

"You think?" I said, my interest in attending now piqued.

"Of course. The killer won't tell the truth about its whereabouts, but someone else who doesn't have anything to hide, might just share."

"That does sound like a good idea," I said.

"And, they always say that the killer comes back to the funeral," she added

"Who is 'they'?"

"The people... they... You know. People who solve murders."

I chuckled. "Okay. Well, if they say we should, I guess we should."

She waved a hand at me. "We can keep a look out and listen

for any clues from all the people there."

"That's a lot of looking out and listening in for two people."

"I'll get the Roble Belles to help us."

"Did you tell them about this?"

"Of course I did."

My phone rang and saved Auntie from me fussing at here. I really was going to have to talk to her about not telling everything she knew.

It was Alex.

I glanced over at Auntie, she would be all in my conversation, but I wanted to talk.

I knew I'd probably regret doing it in front of her.

"Hello," I said, connecting, trying not to let on to Auntie who it was.

"Hey, baby," he said. "I've been busy all in day in the seminars."

"I wondered why I hadn't heard from you. You knew I was worried about your exposure to the poison."

"I'm good. I'll be better if I can see you," he said. "How about dinner tonight?"

"You're coming here?" I asked.

"I was thinking we could meet somewhere halfway in between?"

"Okay," I said.

"Are you around your auntie?" he asked.

"Yep."

"I could tell," he said. "Look, I'll ask around here for a nice place between here and there and I'll text you the address and time."

"Sounds good," I said.

"Can't wait to see you."

"Me either," I said, a blush coming over my face.

"Okay. Bye."

"Bye."

"Who was that?" Nosy-Zanne asked as soon as I got off the

phone.

"A friend."

"You don't have any friends."

"Well, if that wasn't a punch in the gut," I said.

"Was it Chief-of-Staff?"

"I thought we agreed about the name."

"You didn't let me finish," she said. "I was going to say, Chief-of-Staff Alex."

"We're going out to dinner tonight."

"Do you want me to make a batch of tea for you to give him?"

"No."

"Good," she said, and blew out a breath acting relieved, "because I don't think I have anything powerful enough to get that man on the right track."

Chapter Twenty-One

Dinner with Alex turned out good. A small Italian restaurant in Jasper, only a forty-five minute drive for me, a little over an hour for him. The food was scrumptious, the atmosphere in the restaurant inviting. I didn't try so hard to get "gussied up" as Auntie Zanne put it. A pair of sensible pumps, a deep purple lace dress, and a simple pair of gold earrings. I looked pretty, I thought, but didn't look like I was trying. The rest of me was what it was, my hair and skin is what it is, and good or bad, Alex didn't say a word about it.

"You're looking good," I said to him. "Face all cleared up. Pain gone away?"

"Sure is."

"Stomach better?"

"Everything's better now that I'm here with you."

He wore an Italian virgin wool, light gray suit I'd bought him. If he did it to impress me, it worked. A light gray shirt, a gray silk tie with diamond shapes peppered throughout. His low-cut hair, short beard and moustache recently trimmed and lined. I pictured him venturing out in St. Charles to find a barber. It all made me smile.

I thoroughly enjoyed his company, and it seemed he enjoyed mine. It seemed as if we fell right back into sync with each other, the way it had been before I moved back to Roble. We talked, laughed, we touched and it seemed like a warmth of tenderness surrounded us.

"And this is the second murder now," I said, telling him how the little place I'd avoided was becoming almost as exciting as the metropolis I'd been pining for.

"Well, let's hope that crime here never gets as bad as it is in Chicago," he said.

"Fingers crossed," I said and held up my hand, one finger wrapped around the other.

"So you solved the first one and now are kind of undercover on this one?"

"Yeah, because if my cousin, Pogue, ever found out that I was meddling in his investigation, I think he'd burst a membrane."

"Burst a membrane?" He threw his head back and laughed. "It's not taking you long to pick up the slang down here."

I suddenly felt defensive. "Being *down* here. Or *from* down here, isn't a bad thing," I said. Shrugging, I added, "I am what I am."

"Okay, Popeye," he said, holding up his hands. "I like what you are." He reached over and took my hand. "I love what you are."

I smiled. At least outwardly. On the inside there was more that I wanted to say to him, but couldn't. Or wouldn't. Or was afraid to.

But it nagged at me, and nagged some more. I wanted to make the night enjoyable, so all during dinner I didn't say anything. I just didn't know when I'd see him again, and I didn't want our last words to be angry or bitter ones, or with me whining about anything. But by the time the dessert menu was brought over, I just couldn't keep quiet anymore. He was leaving. My heart was aching and I didn't know where I stood. I didn't know what I was waiting on.

"Did you think I was just going to run off without saying anything?" Alex said, when I told him I wasn't sure if I was going to hear from him again when he left that night.

"You did," I said. "I thought you'd be there when I got back."

"I started feeling better, and I knew I had to drive to Lake Charles the first thing..." He looked at me. "Plus, I was hungry. We missed dinner and I hadn't eaten all day. I grabbed a bite to eat and then, you know, I just wanted to get some rest. In a bed."

"You were in a bed."

"My hotel bed, you know what I meant."

"So what is going on with us?" I took my fork and picked over the chocolate truffle cake I'd ordered. I had let my coffee get cold.

"The same thing that's been going on with us," he said.

"No, it's not the same. Before you were married. We had to keep us a secret."

"Well that part has changed," he said, and smiled "That's good, right?"

"Has it?"

"Of course it has," he said. "I wasn't trying to keep it a secret when I rented a car and drove nearly two hours to see you, was I?"

"I don't know."

"You don't know?" He took in a breath, and I wasn't sure if he was irritated with me, or just wanting me to understand. "Look, Romaine. We're just going to have to tough out this long-distance relationship until we can get back to Chicago."

"Is that still the plan?" I asked.

"Still my plan. I'm doing all I can, calling folks that owe me favors. But we can't make a job appear out of thin air. It's not me. It's the economy."

I chuckled. "That's funny."

"What?"

"The economy is keeping us apart."

"Nothing can keep us apart," Alex said. "Unless you don't want to be with me anymore."

I smiled.

"Look," he said. "You can pack up right now and come back with me. Stay at my house and we can work this out. Coming here... Staying here seems to be what you want."

"I just don't want to have to count on you for everything I need."

"I don't mind."

That made a cover of warmth enfold me and the words seemed

all I needed to hear.

"Everything will be fine," he said. "You'll see."

I had begun to wonder what it was going to take for me to be fine. I made the decision to come back to Roble because I didn't have a place to stay. Now he was offering one to me. Why wasn't I jumping at the opportunity? Wasn't it what I wanted? Wasn't it what I'd been hoping for all this time? Maybe Auntie and her marriage tropes had made me anxious about what a marriage to Alex would be. I closed my eyes, took in a breath and when I opened them, I put on a smile.

I had been so foolish for so long, wanting someone else to bring me the happiness I craved. He was right. Everything was going to be fine. I was going to be fine. And then suddenly I knew, only I could make sure of that.

There was a *thump, thump, thump* which made me bounce in my seat, and I knew exactly what it was. I had a flat tire.

"Of course," I said and hit the palms of my hands on the steering wheel after pulling over to the side of the road and taking the car out of gear. "Of course."

I was driving back from my dinner with Alex, feeling sad, and free, and frustrated, and relieved, and happy, and lovesick, and heartbroken, all at the same time.

I took in a breath.

So, instead of going straight home, I took a now-frequent detour and drove by the new ME facility. I loved that place—so shiny and new, it made me so happy that I'd drive by just to look at it, but tonight it was the reason for my current crisis. If I'd gone straight home, I wouldn't have been on this country road that clutched in its black sea of asphalt something which could puncture the tread of my tire.

I grabbed my white-background, floral print pashmina out the backseat I'd brought to guard against the chill of the evening, got out of the car, wrapped it around me and circled the car. It was the back tire, driver's side, flat as day old Pepsi. I didn't know if getting air would get me home or if it required a tire change. Either way, it wasn't something I could currently do myself.

Auntie had an auto service she used for her cars, but I didn't know the number or even if she used the same service that I remembered. I pulled out my phone and called the roadside assistance I had with my cell provider. I'd given up my car long ago, but I always played it safe and kept the service as part of my mobile plan. I just didn't like ever being stuck somewhere without help. They took my information quickly and efficiently and estimated a twenty-minute wait. I knew they'd probably be much longer.

The first question they asked was if I was in a safe place. I was on a dark, desolate country road, the nearest clearance about half a mile away. That clearing was the ME facility. I told them yes, I was safe and gave them the address to the office, letting them know that that was where they'd find me when the tow truck arrived. I was going to hike down the road and wait inside.

So glad I didn't wear the five-inch heels.

I'd walked the Lakefront Trail on a regular basis the entire time I lived in Chicago, and after all I was raised a country girl. Walking the three thousand feet or so to the facility shouldn't even work up a sweat.

I couldn't see my hand in front of my face in the dark night. It was quiet and cool out, I stuck my phone down into my evening bag and put the gold chain strap over my body and pulled my shawl up over my shoulders. I paced my steps as I walked, keeping to the side, careful not to stumble on any loose pebbles.

I soon learned it wasn't the loose pebbles that I needed to worry about. Along my mostly always-deserted road came a truck. First, the 4x4 approached at regular speed, but then seemed to slow as if it recognized me. I didn't want to be bothered with anyone and didn't mind the time I had to spend waiting for a tow truck. I decided if a window came down and I was asked if I needed help, I was going to wave it off and tell them I was okay. Help was on the way. But then it stopped. A good twenty-five feet from me as if it were watching me. Motor revving, breaking through the silence of the night, a flicker of the headlights and it went to high beam. I held up my hand to shield the glare, and turned my head away.

"What do you want?" I mumbled to myself, my heart starting to race. I hadn't ever imagined that I'd become afraid of anything I'd encounter when I stepped out of my car. Now I knew that if something happened, no one might come to look for me down this road. It wasn't the way back from Jasper where'd I told Auntie Zanne I was going, and there were no houses down it either way.

"Why are you just sitting there," I muttered. My head was starting to ache with fear, my legs tingling, my hand trembling. I slowed my pace, now anxious about me moving nearer to it rather than the other way around.

The revving stopped, I could hear the truck being put into gear and then it took off. It came racing down the road my way. I stood still, bracing myself. I couldn't determine which way it might go, so I didn't know which way to run. I took in a deep breath and held it.

The truck stayed in its lane as it *whooshed* past me, blowing my hair and pashmina up and out. I turned and watched it as it passed. Black maybe. Dark-colored for sure. There was lettering on the back windshield. A long name. Maybe the word "University" was part of it. I couldn't tell. Hurrying my eye to the back of the truck to see the license plate, I saw a decal of a fleur-de-lis. Blue. Maybe. Yellow. Definitely. The colors caught my eye and made me miss most of the numbers of the plate. I remembered a zero. I think a one.

"Shoot!"

I quickened my steps and, licking my lips, I tried to calm myself. I could see the facility. Big. Dark. Safe. I turned back to look down the black road where the truck had disappeared. I swallowed hard, turned face forward and broke into a trot. Picturing myself on the dark road in a horror flick, I thought perhaps my heart may explode it was beating so hard. Then I heard the roar of the truck again. Coming back my way.

I needed to hide.

I stumbled down the small embankment at the road's side, taking the brightly colored pashmina off and balling it up. Everything else I had on was dark, it would meld into the night. I was hoping to get lost in all the blackness that surrounded me. I laid flat in the grass and tried not to even breathe. The truck came slowly back down the road, taking its time, seemingly searching for me. I closed my eyes and waited.

The minute or so seemed like an eternity. I wanted to try to get the license number, but was too afraid to lift up my head.

And then it left.

As soon as I knew it was gone, I got up and ran to the building. Out of breath and carrying my shoes, I shakily pushed in the code on the keypad and pulled the door open when I was showered in the glow from headlights.

I hurried in and shut the door knowing no one could get to me once inside. But as I pulled it closed, I saw that it was a car—a Cadillac, not the truck that had pulled in. I squinted my eyes. "Ball 1" was the license plate. It was one of Auntie's cars.

I watched through the glass door as Rhett stepped out of the car door.

I pushed the door open, happy to see him. "What are you doing here?" I asked, tears starting to well up in my eyes.

"I came to see about you," he said. He stood at the door and then looked me over. "Are you okay?"

"I am now," I said. "I am now."

Chapter Twenty-Two

Since I'd gotten back to Roble, Rhett seemed to have a habit of showing up when I needed something. I had decided to paint my room solo, and he appeared at my door and offered the help of he and his bandmates. I needed a ride to a place Auntie wanted me to come, I was going to ask him after I grabbed a bite to eat, and he showed up while my head was sticking in the refrigerator. At the wedding when I couldn't find Auntie or her Roble Belles and needed help clearing people out, there he was.

It seemed like that's what he did for me. Show up.

"You're always showing up," I said, my questions about him rising. Auntie thought he was undercover, and maybe part of what he was doing included watching me. How else could he always seem to know when I needed help?

No, I thought. Who uses their real name when they do that? I looked at him. Maybe his name wasn't really Rhett. And maybe that's why he'd always been so secretive.

"How did you know I was here?" I asked.

"You were taking a long time getting back," he said. "I know that you come by here."

"Did Auntie Zanne tell you to come and look for me?"

"Maybe," he said, drawing the word out.

"Or maybe not?"

He looked at me, then turned his head to glance back out into the dark night.

"Was someone after you?" he asked, turning back to me.

"What makes you think that?" I asked.

He pointed to my dress. "It's stained down the front like you pressed yourself against the ground, lying flat. If you had fell, you'd be more scuffed up."

"I got a flat tire," I said. "I'm waiting for roadside service."

He turned and looked outside again. "Where is the car?" he asked.

"Down the road. About half a mile."

"And you walked from there?"

"Yes."

"And is that when someone came after you?"

"You want to come in?" I asked. "Or just stand here at the door."

"I can come in. It'll be nice to see the place that occupied all your time over the last few months."

We walked over to the desk, and sat. He took one of the chairs on the opposite side of the desk. I took my phone out of my purse and laid it on the table so I could watch for it ringing. With all the antics going on outside, I didn't have any gauge how much time had passed.

"So you want to tell me what happened when you were walking from the car here?"

"I don't."

"Why?"

"Because there isn't much to tell. I don't know much. I was walking here and a truck seemed to be... I don't know stalking me."

"The truck was stalking you?" he asked, a smirk on his face.

I hunched a shoulder. "The driver in the truck, I guess would be the stalker."

"Did you see who it was?"

"No. I didn't see anyone. I'm not even sure of the color of the truck, so I can't describe it to you. I didn't get the license plate number, and I can't be sure any of it was as menacing as I thought at the time."

"Just menacing enough for you to hit the ground and hide?"

"Just about that much."

"You want me to take a look at your flat tire? I can fix it"

"No, roadside service shouldn't be long now," I said, I touched my phone to bring up the time. "They said twenty minutes."

"Well, I'll stay with you until you get back home. Follow you after they repair the tire. Keep you safe."

"You're going to keep me safe?"

"Yep. I'll keep you safe for as long as you'll let me."

"What's your real name?" I said, looking at him out the side of my eye.

"What kind of question is that?" he said and chuckled. "And where did it come from?"

"Remmiere is a French name, right? You speak French. Not French Creole, but you're not from France."

"Are you suspecting me of being the killer again?" he said. He shifted in his seat so he could look at me. "Remember you thought I might have killed Herman St. John and put his body in a casket at Babet's funeral home."

"His real name was Ragland Williamson, but you know that, don't you?"

He raised an eyebrow.

"And of course I remember I thought you did that," I said. "To be honest if I hadn't been the one to figure out who the real killer was, I might still believe you were the one who did it."

"What? Why?"

"Because you're so secretive."

"I am not," he said. "Ask me anything, I'll tell you."

"Do you have a home? Because you're always at our place."

"Yes, I have a home. Would you like to see it? I can take you there now."

"No. I don't want to see it. And don't change the subject."

"Sorry," he said. "Next question."

"Are you a spy?"

"No." A slight chuckle erupted from the back of his throat. "Didn't we have this conversation before, the day I helped paint your room?"

"You remember that?"

"I remember everything that has to do with you," he said.

"Back to my questions."

"Okay." He made a solemn face, indicating he was going to be serious and cooperate.

"You're not here in Roble to spy on my Auntie?" I asked.

He shook his head. "Nope."

"What about me?" I said.

"What about you?" he repeated.

"Are you here to spy on me?"

"Not officially."

"What does that mean?"

He smiled. "I plead the fifth. Next question, please."

"Are you working undercover on a sting operation?"

"A sting operation?" He frowned and shook his head. "Why would I be here on a sting operation?"

"See," I said. "You didn't answer the question. You're always sidestepping things."

"I'm going to answer it, I just wondered where that came from."

"It came from me. My mouth. My brain."

"Oh. Well, for you, your mouth and brain, the answer is no."

"Then what are you doing here?"

"I'm hanging out with you until your roadside service arrives."

"I mean in Roble."

"Just like you," he said and blew out a breath. "I'm running away from my life."

Chapter Twenty-Three

I'd been up since the crack of dawn.

It was the day of the Bumper's funeral, but Auntie didn't want to waste one minute of daylight. She wanted to go over to Angel's Grace to start getting it ready for the awards dinner during homecoming weekend. And her shrill voice flooding the air up the steps and into my room served as a zealous, annoying alarm clock.

"Why do you have to do it this morning?" I said, yawning. I stumbled into the kitchen to get a caffeine rush to kick start my day. "And what are you doing here?" Rhett was sitting at the table, doing his usual. Eating.

"Good morning to you, too," he said, a lump of food in his jaw.

"Be nice to Rhett," Auntie said. She was standing at the stove, stirring in a pot. "He came to help."

"What other reason would he be here?" I asked. "Isn't that his job?"

"Romaine Gabriela Sadie Heloise Wilder!" Auntie said. "By all that is Holy, I did not raise you to be so rude. Or, condescending."

"It's okay, Babet. I know she appreciates me."

I couldn't help but to smile because that was true.

"What are you two up to?" she said.

"I guess Romaine should tell you that."

"What Romaine?"

"I had a flat tire last night."

"It was a little more than that."

I frowned. I didn't want to worry her, plus maybe since it was dark and late, I might have thought I was in more danger than I had been. Even perhaps I thought a little more happened than really did.

"What happened, Rhett?"

"She got ran off the road by some anonymous truck."

"I didn't get ran off the road," I said.

"Did she?" Auntie looked at Rhett.

"That's what she told me," he said, smiling. I guess he enjoyed having me and auntie at odds.

"That's not exactly what happened," I said. "I got a flat. And," I wanted to turn the table on Rhett, "he showed up out of nowhere. I think he follows me, Auntie."

"Well, I could think of worse things," she said.

Rhett winked at me.

"I think it's kind of scary," I said.

"You need to lay off the coffee," she said and pointed at my cup. "It's making you paranoid."

"Did you wake me up this early to abuse me?"

"No," she said. "I need your help."

"Need your help," I said at the same time.

"We need to make a run over to Angel's Grace. We need to take over the mums and meet the caterer so I can show her the kitchen where she'll prepare the food.'

"You're just now getting the caterer?" I said. "This close to the dinner?"

"We had to change caterers. The one I had was hired to do the repast after the services today, too. She said she couldn't do both in one week," Auntie said.

"Wasn't she contractually obligated to you?" I said.

"And what did you suggest I tell her?" Auntie said. "That if she did the repast I was going to sue her for breach of contract?"

"I guess that wouldn't be a good thing."

We left and went over to Angel's Grace. It was just me and Auntie, Rhett stayed at the house. I didn't know why he had been there so early if he hadn't come to help us.

Auntie met the Roble Belles there and the caterer. She had me walk the hall, while she dictated where the decorations would go, where to store the mums for the people on the dais, and showed the kitchen to the caterer.

I saw no reason I should be there.

Chapter Twenty-Four

Auntie Zanne wore her navy blue, double-breasted funeral service suit. She had donned her complete funerary attire—white cloth gloves, nude stockings and black one-inch heel pumps. She stood, back parallel to the wall near the front of the church. Hands behind her back, nodding without a change in her facial expression as people walked up to view the casket, even directing with a wave of hand if they faltered, indicating for them to move along. If one didn't know any better, it was easy to believe that Ball Funeral Home had been put in charge of the arrangements.

And then there were her "lieutenants" the Roble Belles. They were peppered out among the congregation. Walking up and down the aisles, talking, smiling nodding—taking in information I guess. She had given her entourage their orders and they seemed to be on task.

No one said a word to her, tried to remove her from the post she'd taken, said a peep against her, or asked her to call down her Belles. That's how much respect Suzanne Babet Derbinay commanded, even when her actions were dead wrong.

I sat in the back of the church at Auntie's suggestion, I agreed it had the best vantage point. I wasn't sure what I was supposed to be looking for, but I wanted to do a better job than I had at the wedding.

The first thing I noticed was the same organist that had been at the wedding. She had on the same white dress and white fascinator with a birdcage veil which covered her eyes. Her cane leaning against the side of her instrument, she had the same plastered smile and still looking as if she was going to keel over at any minute. Then I saw my cousin, Pogue.

Dressed in his sheriff's uniform, starched and pressed, he stood in the back near the door. He seemed to scrutinize every person who walked past him. He saw me and our eyes locked. No smile for me, I guess that meant he was all business today.

He gave me a curt nod and then headed my way.

"Oh shoot," I mumbled, my heart skipping a beat. I didn't want to talk to him, I was doing exactly what he'd asked me not to do—trying to solve the murder. What if he was there because he was on the same page as Auntie—he thought killers come to the funeral? It would make him more attentive and he'd noticed me talking, well interviewing, possible suspects.

"Hi Romie," he said.

"Hey Pogue," I said, trying to sound chipper, hoping he wouldn't notice the nervousness in my voice.

"What are you doing here?" he asked.

He would ask me that...

"Uhm... You know." I hunched my shoulders. "Paying my respects."

He squinted his eyes at me. "You didn't know him or his family."

"I did know Mrs. Hackett. Sort of."

"Right."

"She used to be in one of Auntie's clubs. Plus, I came with Auntie. She's feeling bad about everything happening at her place."

"You're not poking your nose in, are you?"

"Me?" I said and swallowed hard. I didn't want to lie to my cousin and I had promised myself and made Auntie aware that anything significant I found out, I would share with Pogue. But I didn't know anything yet, so need of upsetting him.

"Yes you. And Babet. I know how she can talk people into doing things."

"I told you, she can't talk me into doing anything I don't want to do."

Which was true, only thing was investigating the murder was something I did want to do.

"Okay," he said. "Just remember, please, to let me handle this."

"Handle away," I said and let out a slight chuckle.

"Why are you here?" I asked.

"I heard that the killer often comes to the funeral."

"You think he, or she, is here now?" I said. I swung around to take a gander at the crowd.

"I would I know," he said and let out a huff. "It's a silly idea. What difference does it make if the killer does come when I have no idea who the killer is?" He shook his head. "It was a ridiculous idea."

"I guess that makes sense," I said, even though it was the reason I was there.

"I'm the law. I can have any of these people come down to the station and speak to me. I've been standing here watching people as they stream in, and for what? Is the killer just going to stand up and announce his deed?" He laughed out loud. "I'm leaving." He touched my arm. "See you later."

"See you," I said.

Perhaps Pogue was right. How do you pick out a murderer in a room full of people? I turned and faced the room. I let my eyes scan the faces. Did any of them look like a killer?

I couldn't tell.

Mr. and Mrs. Hackett were sitting on the first row pew. I knew they hadn't done it. Leastways, I hoped they hadn't.

Both had red eyes, but weren't crying. They sat quietly and to themselves. It was the first I'd seen of Mr. Hackett since the day of the wedding. He wore the same expression, bewilderment, as if he didn't exactly know why he was there. He didn't sit next to his wife, but at the end of the pew and nodded at whomever came by without saying a word. Gaylon, the niece we'd met the other night, sat to one side of Mrs. Hackett, a box of tissue ready in hand, just in case the tears did start to tumble. On the other side sat Jorianne.

From what I could tell, Mrs. Hackett liked her son's choice. I'd noticed how she referred to her as "Jori," not a familiarity I'd heard others take. And Jorianne seemed to cling to Mrs. Hackett for comfort and support. Mr. Alvarez, Jorianne's father sat next to her. And in the two rows behind them sat what had to be the future linemen for an entirety of future NFL teams. All guys. All big. All with red-rimmed eyes.

The next row didn't yield any faces who were familiar to me. That brought my attention quickly around to where were Piper and Bonnie Alvarez? Seemed like they would be part of the family and sit up front.

The two of them were at the top of my suspect list, and two I felt I should keep my eye on. But they were nowhere in sight. I wondered would I be able to pick up any clues from them even if I could locate them. I didn't have to wonder long.

Piper slid in the pew next to me, her mother next to her.

"We thought we were going to be early," Piper leaned over and whispered to me. "There are so many people here."

The church was packed and the service wasn't scheduled to begin for another fifteen minutes.

I turned to Piper and smiled, then leaned forward and reached a hand toward Mrs. Alvarez. "How are you doing?" I said.

Mrs. Alvarez nodded at me, then pulled a fan from her purse and started to fan herself, not giving the slightest recognition to my gesture.

I pulled my hand back. It was going to take some effort to get a confession out of her.

"I saw Jorianne up with Mrs. Hackett," I said to either one of them that cared to comment.

"Yeah, she rode in the family car." It was Piper who answered. Guess I was going to talk to her.

"Oh," I said. "Did your dad ride with them, too?"

"No. He rode with us. We went to the restroom before finding our seats." She leaned in and smiled. "Didn't want to have to go in the middle of the service, you know." She nodded and sat back up straight. "But Jorianne was up at the crack of dawn," Piper said. "Had everyone else up with her. She didn't want to be late."

"That's understandable," I said.

"First time in her life," Mrs. Alvarez said. "Perhaps one good thing will come out of this."

I leaned forward. "Excuse me," I said, although I'd heard her, I just couldn't believe her words.

Piper whispered, tilting her head toward me. "Probably the first responsible thing Jorianne's done in her life."

I saw Mrs. Alvarez give a curt nod and mumble, "I would do anything to see her more responsible."

"So what do you think about it being murder?" Piper asked me.

"Shhh!" Mrs. Alvarez swatted at her daughter. "Not that conversation here.

"I wonder if it was someone at the wedding," Piper said, ignoring her mother.

"Of course it was," Mrs. Alvarez said, despite her warning. "But no one will ever catch whoever did it. The killer is properly long gone." She nodded, her pronouncement making a search for the killer unnecessary.

"Can you imagine, coming to the wedding, knowing you were going to kill the groom? That's got to give you a rush."

"I don't know if I'd think a rush..." I gave a little snort. "Who do you think did it?"

"Don't answer that, Piper," Mrs. Alvarez said. "That's for the sheriff to figure out."

Piper whispered to me. "It's usually women who like to use poison."

"How do you know he was poisoned?" I asked. That tidbit hadn't been released.

"Don't answer that," Mrs. Alvarez said, then looked up at me. "Can't you find something other to do than egg my daughter on about murder mysteries? It isn't proper to discuss things like that at a funeral."

I would stop asking only her questions, I thought, *if I could get you to talk.*

I sat back to gather my thoughts. I had plenty more questions and if Piper was the only one I could get to answer them, then I was going to continue with her.

Then I spotted the best man. Chase Turner. I needed to talk to him, too, but the sight of him reminded me of something Auntie had said.

I leaned close to Piper and tried to lower my voice enough that her mother couldn't hear me. "Why was Chase," I pointed toward him, "Bumper's best man? He didn't play football with him."

"I don't know why he picked him," Piper said. "None of us hardly know him."

"He was a better choice than those two ruffians he was always running around with." I looked over at Mrs. Alvarez who evidently didn't approve of Boone Alouette or LaJay Reid enough that she thought it was okay to speak about Bumper's choice of Chase at the funeral.

Piper shook her head as if to say don't pay her mother's comment any attention. "Boone told me yesterday that he hadn't been sure if he'd be able to get here because he'd already committed to be here for homecoming. He didn't know if he could afford to make two trips. His family doesn't have a lot of money."

"Neither does yours," Mrs. Alvarez said. "But you or Jorianne can't ever seem to realize that."

Piper rolled her eyes and leaned in closer. "LaJay has a thing for Jorianne." She grimaced. "Probably wouldn't have been a good idea to make him best man."

"He was still in the wedding, though," I said.

"That's because Bumper foolishly wouldn't believe that his friend would try to take his girl," Mrs. Alvarez said. "Now if the two of you could be quiet, they're ready to start the service."

Chapter Twenty-Five

Bumper Hackett was one of Roble's own and the outpouring at the service proved it. Everyone, so went the testimonials, had his back when he suffered from his asthma attacks, cheered him on since he started in football in the peewee league, and waited anxiously to receive their wedding invitation. And from the stories told, it evidently hadn't been unusual for his mother to pass out inhalers to anyone around.

That made it easy for the killer...

The mayor, his high school coach, the Roble Belles, and even the JOY Club had provided Resolutions that were read during the service. All of them claimed to have taken part in all his undertakings and had been filled with immeasurable pride following news about him as he fulfilled his dreams and upon getting recruited to the University of Southern California.

"Hello, I'm Boone Alouette."

"And I'm LaJay Reid."

The two athletes, per the program, were the last two to speak about their friend.

"I knew Bumper better than anyone," Boone said. "We'd been friends since we were kids."

"Yeah he did," LaJay said, leaning into the mic, smiling at his friend. "He knew him longer, but we both loved him the same." He turned and looked at Boone, who nodded in agreement.

Boone took center stage again. "It was just a few days ago that we were all laughing and talking together. I hadn't even thought I'd make it home to the wedding." He shook his head. "And now I am so glad I did so I could get to see my best friend one more time."

"I miss him so much. But I'm sure everyone here who knew him will miss him too. And remember, Mrs. Hackett," Boone said, looking over at her, "LaJay and I are still your sons, not by blood, but we are here anytime you need us."

"We'll always be here for you." LaJay leaned into the mic. "Just like we were for Bumper." The dreadlocked friend looked at the casket, tapped his heart twice with the side of his fist, and said. "We love you, man."

Then together they said, "For the Gold, and for the Navy and White. Rah!"

Those were Roble High colors. The colors they'd worn on their football jerseys every Friday night when the lights went on. Each had gone away to college and wore different colors for their team now, but I assumed they were saying there would always be a bond between them. That brought a lot of tissues to eyes, their words had touched the hearts of the crowd.

During the next few songs, one courtesy of the JOY Club and their overzealous organist, my mind and eyes started to wander. That's when I spotted the best man—Chase Turner. "There you are, I muttered. "I want to talk to you."

"Excuse me," I said sliding past Piper then Mrs. Alvarez. "Sorry." I bumped into Piper's knee. "I need to go to the ladies' room."

Piper gave me a polite smile, but Mrs. Alvarez seemed put out. She made a face and turned her legs to the side with a *hmpf.*

"Sorry," I said again and scooted past her. My heart raced as I tried to push through the standing room only crowd to get to Chase.

He stood back against the wall, holding onto the program that he'd rolled up into a scroll. His eyes weren't focused and he probably couldn't have told anyone what was going on. He didn't seem to be sad, just going through the obligatory motions. I was thinking that he didn't want to be there, he had been elusive—disappearing right when Bumper collapsed, not being at Mrs.

Hackett's house and he hadn't even gone up front during the funeral to speak. I wanted to speak to him before he disappeared again.

"Hi Chase," I said, I started speaking before I even got to him.

"Hi," he said and looked at me as if he was trying to remember who I was.

"Romaine Wilder," I said. "We met at the wedding."

"Oh," he smiled, "I remember. You're a doctor, right?"

I nodded. "I'm a medical examiner."

"The coroner?"

The two weren't exactly the same, but the majority of people thought they were, no need getting into technicalities. "Yes," I said.

"So you're the one that's saying it's murder?"

"I performed the autopsy on Bumper."

"Same thing, right? You're the one who signed the death certificate.

"That would be me."

"Why would you think he was killed?"

"It's not what I think, it's what the evidence has shown me."

"Oh really. So you know how they killed him?"

"They?"

"You know, whoever did it."

"I can't speak on that right now, it wouldn't be my place." I stepped a little closer to him to make our conversation easier. "I was wondering if I could ask you a couple of questions."

"About what?"

"About Bumper."

"Like what?"

"I was just wondering if you knew what happened to the inhaler he had."

"Is that what happened to him?"

"What do you mean?" I asked.

"The inhaler wasn't working?"

"Like I said, I can't really say. I have to wait for the police to release that information."

"I thought it was like public information or something."

I didn't say anything. A funeral already wasn't the best place to question a suspect, and I didn't want to waste my time giving him the same answer over and over. He seemed to understand my silence.

"No, I don't know what happened to it," he said.

"Why did you leave the gazebo?" I wanted to hurry and get through all my questions.

"What?"

"I saw you through the window right when Bumper collapsed standing there with him and my auntie, but you weren't there when we got CPR started."

"I thought the other doctor did the CPR?"

"Dr. Hale." I nodded. "He did. And perhaps I shouldn't have said 'we.'" I gave him a polite smile for catching my use of word after I'd just corrected him. "I was just wondering why you weren't there."

"Well for one thing I wanted to get out of the way, I heard the doctor say he was coming. And second, I'd forgotten the ring."

"The ring?"

"Jorianne's wedding ring. I was so nervous about losing it that I'd locked it up in the glove compartment of my truck. I had gone back to get it. And that's when I saw Piper and she told me he'd fainted or something."

"You and Piper friends?" I asked. I had already heard her answer.

"I guess we're starting to be," he said and shrugged. "I don't live here, so really no need to strike up any kind of relationship—friendship or whatever." He glanced her way.

"When did Bumper ask you to be his best man?" I asked. "You guys hadn't been friends long, had you?"

"No. But he was a good kid and he was just trying to do the right thing. Trying to show me he could, at least."

"What was the right thing?" I asked.

He shook his head. "It really doesn't matter now. There's

nothing that can be done about it. He didn't even get the chance to tell me everything."

"Something was bothering him?"

He shrugged. "Yeah. I guess. But it's not bothering him anymore."

Chapter Twenty-Six

The service was over and the pastor had announced that the family and friends could take another look at the body. I found Auntie Zanne. She stopped wearing her funeral director's hat and switched to congregationalist. She was chatting and hugging everyone who passed by her.

"Auntie," I said, pulling her away. "Did the Roble Belles find out anything?"

"They haven't reported back yet," she said.

"Okay," I said. "Well, I spoke with Mrs. Alvarez, Piper and Chase."

"And?"

"And they're still at the top of my suspect list."

"All three?"

"Yes. All three." I gave a firm nod. "And isn't that the same organist who was at the wedding?" I was thinking that maybe she was someone we should speak to. She'd been up at the frontline of all the happenings the entire time.

"Yes," she said. "That's Miriam Colter, member of the JOY Club, she's our go-to organist."

"She sure gets around," I said. "I was thinking of speaking to her, but it looks like she might fall over at any minute. Maybe I should wait."

"She always looks like that," she said. "She'll be fine as long as a breeze doesn't push through."

"Is that all it would take—a breeze?"

"Maybe even less. But she is not one to mess with, she's as mean as a snake and sneaky as a cat. Don't worry, though, I already asked her if she remembered seeing what happened to Bumper's inhaler... Oh! Look a-there." Her face lit up, and her attention was diverted mid-sentence. "It's Rhett. He must be here as part of his sting operation." She leaned in close to me and spoke in a barely audible voice. "I knew he'd be here to scope out the people attending. Told you it was the thing to do."

"If he had a sting going, he wouldn't have to scope, he'd already know," I said. "It would be the people he was investigating, and he wouldn't have come after it was over."

"Who is that with him?" Auntie said, ignoring my observation, and pointing. She tried standing on toes to get a better look.

I looked in the direction she'd pointed. It was the first time I'd seen Rhett completely dressed in a suit. Usually by the time I saw him, he'd have changed into a pair of jeans and his ratty tennis shoes. And, again I had to concede, he looked handsome.

Very handsome.

But what Auntie wanted me to take note of was the woman that came in with him, and that made something jiggle in my stomach and dry up the saliva in my mouth.

She was a pretty woman. Younger than me, I could tell, with thick brown hair that wasn't the least bit frizzed, and even thicker eyelashes. Her skin was smooth, even without makeup, an olive complexion that just seemed to glow. The two of them had a familiarity about them that would seem to transcend a working relationship.

And I couldn't figure out why I cared.

"C'mon," Auntie said. "Let's go find out who she is," she sidled up next to me and grabbed my arm. "Try not to act too jealous."

I grunted and made a face. "That hadn't even crossed my mind."

"I don't think you have to worry," she said. "She's probably the other half of his sting operation."

"Hi," Auntie Zanne said as we got over to them.

By that time she was practically pulling me. I just didn't care to meet this woman. I tried to think about Alex, but that didn't seem to work. All I could focus on was her face.

"I'm Babet," Auntie was saying, her voice to me now seemed it came from a vacuum. "Are you a friend of Rhett's?"

"This is Hailey Aaron," Rhett said, smiling one of the smiles when the gold flecks in his eyes twinkled. "Hailey, I told you about Babet. Remember? I work for her. And this is..."

I didn't know if he was getting ready to introduce me or not, but suddenly I didn't care one bit about my ingrained southern manners—I didn't want to meet her so I turned and walked away.

Chapter Twenty-Seven

I didn't have anywhere to go. I'd come in the car with Auntie, and until she finished socializing, I couldn't even get into the car. But the further I got away from flawless Hailey Aaron, the better I felt.

I gave one last look their way and turned back and ran smack into Piper, Boone and LaJay.

"Hi," I said.

"Hi again," Piper said. "You were driving my mother crazy! I loved it."

"I didn't mean to do that," I said. "I just had a few questions stuck in my brain."

"Because you're trying to figure out who killed Bumper?" LaJay asked.

"That's for the police to do," I said. I smiled at the young men. "I think that the both of you did a nice job eulogizing your friend."

"Thanks," they said nearly in unison.

"They have been so good to the family," Piper said. "I wonder did Bumper know what good friends he had."

"He would've done the same for us," Boone said.

"Boone was at the hospital when we all got there," Piper said. "Helping Mrs. Hackett getting everything together, going in the back to get info for them and then comforting her."

"I only made it there before everyone else because when Mr. Hackett got there he was just too upset to drive," Boone said.

"I've never seen Mr. Hackett like that," LaJay said. "He always was so big and strong."

"Yeah, I know," Boone said. "It was scary, and then Mrs. Hackett." He shook his head. "She's always been like a mother to us and to see her so upset was heartbreaking."

"Yeah," Piper said, "it was heartbreaking."

"We're doing a tribute at Homecoming to Bumper," LaJay said "We're hoping Boone can get back for it."

"I'm gonna try," Boone said. "I wasn't sure I could do it and the wedding, so I picked the wedding, but now..." he shook his head. "I'on know, man. This is so messed up."

"Yeah, it is," LaJay said.

"Yes, I heard you weren't even sure at first if you could come," I said. "Is that why you weren't the best man?"

Boone nodded. "Yeah," he said. "Bumper didn't know if he could count on me to be here."

"Where do you two know Chase Turner from?" I said. "The one who was the best man."

"We don't really know him," LaJay said and shrugged.

"He was a friend of Bumper's from California. They met on campus, I think," Boone said. "I don't know how good of friends they were, though."

"Must be pretty good buddies if Bumper asked him to do it," I said.

"It's a shame," Piper said, chiming in. "Come all the way here to be in wedding for a guy you hardly know and he dies on you."

"Right?" LaJay said, agreeing.

"I mean, I just can't believe what happened," Boone said, pushing a finger into his still red eye. "And it's even harder to believe someone did it to him on purpose. I just knew he was having an asthma attack."

"Yeah," LaJay said. "And I didn't think asthma was going to do it, his mother made sure we protected him."

"With all the inhalers?" I asked.

"Yeah," Boone said. It was the first time I'd seen his face brighten. "She used to make us take one whenever we went out to play when we were little. And then she used to hide 'em in places she knew we went to play. There're probably still some out and around that we never found."

"Yeah, I remember Bumper telling me about that," LaJay said.

"Yeah, and Bumper hated it, too," Boone said. "He did not want to ever be sick." Boone shook his head. "He'd say I know what makes me sick, and you know so we can take care of everything without her. I'm not a baby." Boone made a face like he was pouting as he relayed his story.

"That's funny," LaJay said. Then looked around the group. "Oh! Not funny that it made him die, funny how Mrs. Hackett acted."

"Asthma didn't kill him," Piper said. "And it seems like it might take a while for us to find out what did." She gave me a look.

"It's alright, ma'am," LaJay said, directing his eyes toward me. "We understand you can't tell us. I was just saying, you know, why? Why would someone want to kill Bumper?" He shook his head. "Who would do it?"

"My mother might," Piper said. "I heard her tell my father she wanted Bumper out of Jorianne's life."

"She said that?" LaJay said, his eyes wide, seemingly excited about that possibility.

"That's not nice to go blaming your mother," Boone said. "This is serious, isn't it Dr. Romaine?"

I'd never heard anyone call me that. I thought it was cute, but it didn't distract me from Piper's comment. That had given me pause. I remembered something about Bonnie Alvarez wielding a "shotgun" to force them get married.

"I heard she brought a gun to the wedding," I said. God I hated gossip, but it sure was coming in handy at the moment.

"My mother carries a gun everywhere she goes. She loves that little snub-nose Smith & Wesson. You must not be from Texas," Piper said and looked at me. "Everyone carries a gun. Anyway, Jorianne was just wanting to show off, as usual, when she said our momma had lit a fire under Bumper. He wanted to marry her. He didn't need a gun to make him."

"But your mother didn't want Jorianne to marry Bumper?" I asked.

"Nope. Said she could take care of the baby, she and my daddy, Jorianne didn't need no husband. I just think she didn't want Jorianne to move to California."

"She can stay in Texas," LaJay said. "She'll have all the help she needs."

"Man," Boone said and lightly punched his friend, "what I tell you about trying to hit on Jori?" He shook his head. "You're such a rat."

"I thought you said we were going to take care of Bumper's baby?"

"Yeah, well, not like you thinking," Boone said.

"Did any of you see what happened to Bumper's inhaler?" I asked.

"Which one?" Boone asked.

"The one he had with him at the altar."

"I didn't," Boone said.

"I didn't either," LaJay added.

"I did," Piper said. "The best man had it. Chase. He put it in his pocket when we were waiting for the ambulance."

"What happened to you?" Auntie Zanne said. She came up behind me and pulled me out of the conversation I was having with Piper, Boone and LaJay, and walked me out of their earshot.

"I had to question our suspects. And guess what I—"

"You just walked away when Rhett was trying to introduce you to his friend," she said cutting me off. "I know I taught you better manners than that."

"His friend?" I said, my dry mouth coming back.

"Not that kind of friend," she said. "She—her name is Hailey Aaron in case you missed it—is from his hometown. Houston."

"How do you know what kind of friend she is?" I asked.

"Why do you care?" she asked.

"I don't."

"Anyway, I think that was just their front. She's working on that sting with him. I'd be willing to bet."

I rolled my eyes.

"She asked me about Angel's Grace."

"So?"

"So that's where I've got the Mighty Max stored and the information on that bogus scholarship Shane Blanchard wanted me to help him set up. But I know it's all a front for his illegal activities."

"You don't know that," I said, ready to change the subject. "You never told me what Miriam Colter said about the inhaler."

"Look," she said, distracted again. She'd spotted someone else. I figured I'd just have to wait to get home to try and question her on what, if anything, she found out.

"Look at what?"

"That's Shane and Coach Buddy right there."

"Right where?"

"There." She pointed. "Now you want to tell me what they're doing here?"

"I don't know, but I bet you have a guess."

"You bet I do. They probably came to see if Bumper is really dead."

I didn't want to chuckle at a funeral, but I felt one about to erupt.

"What?" I asked, amused. "They thought it might all be a charade, funeral and all, just to catch them?"

"They are criminals and that's what criminals do. And," she said, a look on a face like a light bulb went off, "this is their warning to anyone else if they turn them down. They just wanted to make sure everyone got the message."

"Oh wow," I said.

"Oh no!" she said and ducked behind me. "They're coming over here."

I stepped aside. "They won't kill you here."

"They might," she said, she grabbed my sleeve and pulled me next to her. "They're despicable desperados."

"Mrs. Derbinay," one of them said, walking up to us. "It's nice to see you, so sorry it was under such sad circumstances."

Chapter Twenty-Eight

The conversation with Shane Blanchard and Coach Buddy was as benign as dead skin on the heel of a foot. After two minutes of boring cordiality among the three of them, I excused myself, more politely this time, and waited for Auntie by the car.

She finally came out, all smiles, but I refused to let her expression pique my interest in what else the three of them talked about. Her murder theory, to me, was all silly speculation.

After making an appearance at the funeral, we didn't go to the repast after the service, Auntie was still reeling over not being entrusted to ready Bumper for his eternal rest and refused to socialize.

"I've paid my respects," she said. "And what I want to break is not bread."

When we got home, J.R. met us at the door. He followed me upstairs and Auntie went to the kitchen, she said, to make her a bite to eat.

When I checked my email, I was surprised to see a message from the TxDPS. I clicked on it, knowing it could only be one reason the Texas Department of Public Safety could be emailing me.

But that was so quick.

Sure enough it was their Criminal Investigations Division. I let my eyes scan the sheet, looking for the information I wanted to know. What killed Bumper? But when I read that line, my breath caught in the back of my throat and a chill ran up my spine. I couldn't believe what I saw. I stared at it. Scrolled up then back, thinking it might change. But it didn't.

Then I realized I didn't know anything about that poison. I'd heard that some woman from Texas had sent ricin to the president and the mayor of New York a while back. But that was it. I typed the word into a browser and started my research. I checked out the symptoms first. There were listed differently for ingestion, inhalation and skin and eye exposure. It easily covered Bumper and Alex's symptoms. If you knew what you were looking for.

Then I wondered if I knew we could have saved Bumper. I clicked on "Treatment."

No antidote. *Geesh!*

We probably couldn't have saved him even if we had known.

I clicked back to my email and hit print on the computer. Maybe the toxicology report would be different if I was holding it in my hand. I pulled it off the printer, walked over to my bed and sat down, tugging tightly at the edges of the paper and staring down at it.

"I've got to tell Pogue," I said. "And then get this over to him." I looked around on the bed for my phone, then underneath it. "Where did I put that thing?" I rarely needed it. Auntie's proclamation ringing true in my ear, I didn't have any friends. Then I remembered I had it in my purse, which I left hanging on the doorknob to my room.

"I got the toxicology report back," I said after he picked up. I didn't even give him a 'hello'.

"And were you right?"

I didn't say anything. I knew he knew the answer to that.

"Okay," he said. "Nix that question. What kind of poison was it?"

"Ricin." I plopped down on the bed and stared again at the paper I'd printed out.

"What the heck is that?"

"Comes from the castor bean."

"Is that supposed to tell me what ricin is?"

"The plant that you get castor oil from."

"Castor oil. Jesus. I took that stuff my entire childhood. Are you telling me now it's poisonous?"

"Not the oil, only the protein of the plant. And it's always been poisonous."

"You said before that he inhaled it. Now that you know what it is, you still think that?"

"I do," I said. "Kind of puts things in perspective for me."

"How so?"

"Because there were crumbs on Alex's mouth when he gave Bumper CPR. I wondered where they'd come from."

"Where did they come from?"

"Like I just said, you get ricin from the protein of the plant. It would have to be extracted. Someone—whoever killed him—must have crushed it to get into the inhaler. Maybe it still had small pieces of the castor bean in it, it came up when Bumper inhaled, stuck on his mouth and Alex picked it up."

"That makes sense."

"Only..." I hesitated while I thought it out. "It is making me wonder how it could have been done because ricin takes a while to kill."

"What do you mean 'a while'?"

"Like a couple days. Symptoms come within about four to ten hours. Death, though, might even take up to thirty-six."

"Oh. Jesus," Pogue said. "Is Alex going to die?"

"No," I said, nervousness suddenly bubbling up in me. "Why would you say that?"

"You just said it took a while. I just thought..."

"Don't think like that. Geesh."

"Okay. Okay," he said. "But doesn't that mean somebody fed it to Bumper days before the wedding."

"Maybe." I took in a breath, my words distant. I'd taken to wondering had Alex taken enough of it for it to kill him, too.

"Maybe?"

I thought about the conclusions I'd already made and

everything I'd learned. "I'm sure it was the inhaler, I just don't know when he was introduced to it."

"So tell me how they did it."

"Ricin is deadly as an aerosol, and its water soluble. Someone mixed the albuterol in his canister with ricin. And the symptoms of ricin poisoning when inhaled are shortness of breath, tightness in the chest. Sweating."

"Aren't those the same symptoms as when you're having an asthma attack?"

"Yep," I said. "So no one thought anything different. Not me. Not Alex. Not even Bumper. He probably just thought his asthma wasn't clearing up."

"So I need to find someone who had access to his inhaler," Pogue said.

"Good luck with that," I said. "Everyone at that wedding had an inhaler, and Mrs. Hackett told me she kept them all over the house. Everyone knew that and anyone could have gotten to one."

"Were you questioning Mrs. Hackett, Romie?" He let out a snort. "I asked you not to butt in."

"I didn't question her. I didn't even know he'd been murdered when she told me. She was just upset the inhalers hadn't worked and explained to me how she was always ready with one in case he had an attack. I'm leaving it up to you from here. That's the end of my report. You want to solve it on your own, believe me, you're welcome to it."

I hung up the phone and hung my head. I felt bad for lying to Pogue. I couldn't leave it up to him. Solving that last murder had put a bug inside of me and I couldn't wait to share what I'd just learned with my unlikely ally, Auntie Zanne. I was becoming just like her—lying and conniving.

And on top of that, I wanted to hurry and get off the phone. I needed to check on Alex. Make sure he was alright and let him know what I'd found out.

I just needed to do a little more research first on the poison that killed Bumper and made him sick to get a better idea of what we were dealing with. That part was going to be easy, though, and I wasn't going to need the Internet to do it.

Chapter Twenty-Nine

I took slow, deliberate steps down the stairs and into the kitchen, her usual haunt. I was excited about the information I needed, but if I gave too much away, Auntie would use my energy to feed hers and I'd have to deal with her on overload. I needed her expertise.

My Auntie Zanne was a Voodoo herbalist. In fact, she was the Most High Mambo of the Distinguished Ladies' Society of Voodoo Herbalists. She had a world-wide-web kind of knowledge about plants, herbs and their toxicity right in her white hair-covered head.

"Auntie," I said, planting a kiss on her cheek. She was sitting at the kitchen table, empty glass spice jars set in rows alongside bundles of dried flowers and leaves. "You got a minute?" She was grinding something up in the mortar with her pestle.

"Always for you, Sugarplum." She looked up me at and smiled. "And what you want must be a doozy, you giving me a kiss as a teaser."

"I just think that you're really smart, and I don't know if I ever told you that. Or how much I appreciate you."

"I'm not cooking up any more brews for Alex, if that's what you're wanting," she said. "I'd have to convene a weeklong ritual to command enough power to straighten out that man."

I rolled my eyes.

"I got the toxicology report back," I said, and sat at the table across from her. "I wanted to talk to you about it."

"You did?" she said excitedly. "What was with all the pretense then?" She stood up and wiped her hands and came over to sit next to me. Folding her hands in her lap she leaned into me. "What did they kill him with?"

"Ricin," I said.

"Really," she said. "Oh that's not good."

"You're right," I said. "That's not good. I looked it up and it was used to assassinate some dissident and—"

"Georgi Markov of Bulgaria," she interjected before I could finish my sentence.

"Right," I said. I tilted my head. "I'd never heard of him. How do you know about him?"

"I must have read it somewhere," she said dismissively. "What else you got?"

"Just that it had been thought to have been used in chemical warfare."

"That didn't work out." She said it as if she already knew the answer.

"What?" I chuckled. Something was telling me that she was keeping something from me.

"Nothing. Keep going."

"Nothing else really," I said. "It isn't native to here, meaning the U.S., and I found only one place where it grows here and that's—"

"Griffith Park in L.A."

I leaned back. "Okay, how do you know that?"

"Why wouldn't I know that?" she said.

"Pogue didn't even know what ricin was," I said. "I'd only heard of it, nothing in-depth. I had to look up everything I'm telling you know."

"I have a Ph.D. in plants that can kill you," she said and stood up. She went back to her side of the table.

"There's no such thing, but I know what you mean." I paused and thought about Bumper's cause of death. "Wasn't he the only one that had been in California?" I asked.

"There're lots of people in California, darlin'," she said.

"You know what I mean."

"You thinking it was suicide?"

"No." I thought about my answer I'd just given and realized it wasn't entirely how I felt. "I don't know," I changed my answer to go along with how I really felt, "because I don't know if any of the people at the wedding were in California. And if they were, and brought some back with the purpose to kill him..." I let my voice trail off as I tried to get my thoughts together.

"What?"

"Why didn't they just kill him there?" I shook my head. "Why wait?" I hunched my shoulders. "It doesn't make sense. So maybe he is the one that put it in his inhaler."

"Why would he do that?"

"I don't know." I stared at the wall trying to make my pieces fit together. "Okay. Say that's not what happened."

"It wasn't," she said.

"Say it isn't," I said again, "That means we would need to see who out of our suspects has gone to California recently and knew that the plant grew in Griffith Park."

"They could have gotten it here," she said and tightened her body as if she was waiting for something to hit.

"Here?" I narrowed my eyes at her. "What are you talking about? It doesn't grow here."

"Doc Westin had cancer."

"Don't change the subject," I warned. "And he didn't have cancer." I shook my head. "He died from complications of the flu."

"He didn't tell anybody. Well, not many people."

"That has nothing to do with what we're talking about," I said, getting exasperated. "I want to know how you know about the ricin. You need to tell me that and not digress."

"I'm trying."

"Okay," I said. "So, go ahead." I got up, grabbed a cup and stuck a pod of French Roast in my coffee maker. I leaned back on the counter to wait for it to finish.

"He wanted me to help him look into alternative methods of

treatment," Auntie said. "He came to me for help. So we tried to help him." She turned around in her chair and looked at me. "Did you know ricin had been thought to have positive effects in killing cancer cells?"

"You didn't let him take ricin, did you?" My eyes got as big as saucers. "Is that what really killed Doc Westin?"

"No," she said and waved her hand. Then she cocked her head to one side. "At least I don't think so."

"Oh, Auntie! You don't think so?"

"Well, I wasn't with the man every minute. I can't tell you what he did or didn't do. Or take. But if I had to bet money on it..."

"Who is we?" I interrupted. I needed to know who her accomplices were and try to keep her going in the right direction. She'd digress if I didn't stop her.

"Some of the ladies of the Voodoo Herbalist Society."

"You." I grabbed my coffee, put it up to my mouth blew on it and thought. "Mark. Leonard." I recited the other two I knew.

"Delphine Griffith and Avoyelles Kalty."

"I don't know those two," I said. I walked back over to the table.

"They still exist even if you weren't aware of it."

I shook my head. "Okay, so explain to me how the existence of these people, ricin, and Doc Westin all fit together."

"We all grew it. Well not the doc."

"You can't grow ricin, it's a protein from the castor bean."

"That's what we grew," she said.

"Oh my," I said. I sat down. "So potentially, there's ricin all over Roble?"

"Shelby and Angelina counties, too," she said.

"How did it get there?"

"Delphine Griffith and Avoyelles Kalty."

"That's where they live?"

"Yep."

"Why did so many people grow it?"

"The castor bean isn't native to here, we weren't sure how it would fare. Texas soil and weather conditions are different, so we tried growing it in several different environments."

Okay," I said. "That's good. It means we only need to see who could have gotten it from where it was able to grow."

She scrunched up her nose. "We are very good at what we do."

"So, everyone was successful?"

"Yes."

I let out a huff. I put my elbow on the table and cradled my chin in my hand. "Who knew about it?" I said after a few moments of quiet contemplation.

"I thought no one other than the five of us. I didn't even tell the other herbalists why they were growing it, just that I needed help with cultivating it." She looked at me. "Guess I was wrong about that, huh? 'Cause someone sure found out and killed Bumper with it." She looked at me. "Better question though, is who, other than us, would know what it is and how to use it?"

"Are we going to have to expand our list of suspects to include those four ladies?" I looked at her. "And you?"

"And I'm guessing all the people any of them told about it."

"I thought you didn't tell anyone about it?"

"I didn't."

"Who did you tell?" I figured I'd ask again in a different way. I knew she didn't know the first thing about keeping a secret, she had all but told me that. She hadn't waited a full day to share Piper's announcement about who paid for the caterer with Josephine Gail.

She zipped her mouth shut and held up her right hand. "No one."

I rolled my eyes. "I don't believe that."

"Well, I'm telling you I didn't. I don't know who the other herbalists told. Or Doc Westin. He might have mentioned it to some people. And if he did, those people are the ones you need to look into."

"Why?"

"Everyone else would have said they were growing castor beans, because that's all they knew about it. That's the only thing I asked them to do. Doc Westin's the only one who would have mentioned something about ricin because that's what he wanted it for."

"What happened with Doc Westin?"

"He died."

"No, I mean with the ricin experiment."

"It didn't work."

"Oh my goodness, Auntie. I mean did he actually get any ricin?"

"Why didn't you just say that? I can't read your mind." She took in a breath, her chest heaved up then back down. Her eyes went up like she was thinking. "I don't think so."

She went back to grinding whatever it was in her mortar.

"Auntie," I said.

"What?"

"Can you tell me whatever you know without us having to go back and forth?"

"We grew the castor beans," she said with a huff. "We knew you just can't open up the castor bean and get ricin out. And if you don't get it out the right way, it loses its toxicity."

That made me know that what Alex had ingested, the small piece on his lip, probably wasn't very toxic. It was still entangled in the bean and that wouldn't be enough to kill.

"So are you telling me that Doc Westin wasn't able to get access to any ricin from the castor beans you grew?"

"It'll have a greater potential for killing, whether it's cancer cells or people, if it's been purified by a technical process, and that's difficult for anyone to do. And it's even harder to produce ricin that can be inhaled."

"It sounds like you're reading from a textbook. Just tell me what you're saying."

"It was too hard to use. So we suggested that that not be one of the alternatives he used, unless he wanted to spend time and effort trying to purify it."

"Then what happened?" I asked.

"I don't know." She shook her head. "It's just all such a big mystery."

Chapter Thirty

After I finished talking to Auntie, I went up to my room, J.R. following close at my heels. I was so frustrated with Auntie that I wasn't sure what I'd learned from her would help me solve the case.

Did Doc Westin have ricin or just the castor bean and was unable to extract the deadly protein? And with the information that Auntie Zanne gave me about how hard it was to get, it made me wonder who was sophisticated enough to do it, or the resources to have it done.

I decided to take a little trip and do something I should have done a long time ago. But, first I called Alex and filled him in on all I knew, including the fact that there was no antidote. I also told him that not everyone who ingests it dies. I told him about ricin's extraction process and how that fact alone lessened the chances of him having enough in him to kill him. And, we hadn't noticed any of the symptoms—vomiting, diarrhea, low blood pressure and dehydration. He joked that maybe it was Auntie's tea that saved him. Still we agreed. He should see a doctor.

After I hung up from Alex, I changed into a pair of jeans and a sweater, Texas night air in early October could be a little cool. I tied on a pair of tennis shoes, pulled my unruly hair back into a ponytail, and grabbed my purse.

"Come on, J.R., I've got to go out. I don't know how long I'll be, so you can wait downstairs in your own bed."

I grabbed Auntie's car keys from the wall caddy by the back door, then walked through the front of the house and out of the side entryway to the carport. She usually kept a car and a hearse out for late night runs. I took the car and drove to the ME's office. I wanted to get a look into Doc Westin's boxes because for some reason I kept running into his name.

My little talk with Auntie about ricin had marked the second time Doc Westin's name had come up in our little investigation. The first time with him prescribing medicine for Bumper. I needed to process all she'd told me and see what I could find from what he'd left because for some reason it was really pestering me.

The pharmacist, Mr. McDougal, hadn't thought anything was out of the ordinary when I questioned him about Doc Westin writing prescriptions for the high school's athletes. "He was everyone's doctor," he had said.

I could understand him being the senior of the JOY Club's doctor. He was, after all, in his early seventies, and that made him one of them. Healthcare wasn't always available for their numerous and frequent ailments, nor was it always accessible. But why was he a seventeen-year-old's doctor? At least that's how old Bumper had been in high school. And did he continue to be his doctor once he left for college. How had that worked? Was he just prescribing medicine willy-nilly?

I drove to the parking lot. Three pole lamps illuminated the ME's office. Like death it had odd hours. It was fortuitous that the Commissioners hadn't asked me for my key or changed the code to the security system. They still trusted me with access. Even though it was completed, I could come and go as I pleased, and I really liked that.

I locked the car, punched in the code on the keypad for entry and flicked all the switches on the light panel as I entered. The lights flicked on as I walked across the floor. I had had Catfish store the boxes in a back room until I could get to them. It had only been three or four, but I thought it was better to keep them out of anyone else's view, although besides Auntie and Catfish, no one else had been inside after it was completed.

The Commissioners were going to have to hire staff in addition to a full-time ME, but right now the place's only occupant was me. I lifted one of the boxes marked personal off the top of two other boxes and took it out to the office and sat it on the desk.

I lifted the top of the box and peered inside. What were the odds that I'd pick the right box the first time? In this case zero. The box was filled with personal pictures, desk accessories and periodicals. I put the top back on and went and got another box. That one looked more promising.

It contained a handful of patient files. I pulled them out of the box and took a seat. Some of the names I recognized, some I didn't, but perusing them I was able to note that all of them belonged to people over the age of sixty.

Where was Bumper's file?

Maybe Mr. McDougal had been wrong. He hadn't looked up any records, just gave me information as he remembered it. But when people are familiar to you, sometimes that's all you need. Still it seemed Doc Westin would have something on Bumper, he had it on everyone else.

I started to put the folders back in the box, take it back and grab the next one when I noticed a spiral notebook. It was opened and had Medicare Scam written across the top of the sheet of paper, underlined twice.

"What is this?" I said.

There was a list of names written down one row of the paper. And dates and times in consecutive rows. The dates were more than two years old.

The names matched a lot of the ones that he had file folders for, and notated next to them was JOY. That must be the senior club, I reasoned.

The first entry was almost three years ago: *Two club members, J.D. and M.C. spoke to me about Medicare Part D calls they received. They sent money for insurance coverage, but hadn't received a card. Doesn't sound right!*

I read the next one: *M.C. told me she had several friends who were approached the same way and paid $500 for Part D insurance.*

There were at least a dozen entries like that over the next few pages and when they stopped, Doc Westin had begun making notations that to me seemed to be a detailed account of an investigation.

One of the investigatory notes caught my eye: *I was able to find out a phone number and a name—Chase Turner.*

Chase Turner.

That was the best man's name.

Or maybe not. It might be a common name.

Currently away in military, was written a few entries down.

Well that cleared that right up. I remembered that Chase Turner had worn a military uniform to the wedding.

What did he have to do with a Medicare scam?

I just didn't understand where he fit into all of this, or why he lied to me about not knowing where the inhaler was.

I was sure one didn't have anything to do with the other. And while it might be a good thing to tell Pogue about a Medicare scam, I needed to look for information on ricin and evidence that Doc Westin had written scripts for inhalers for Bumper.

So I closed up the box, took it back and picked up the next one. That box turned out to be what I was looking for.

Inside were at least ten albuterol sulfate inhalation aerosol canisters. The red plastic encasing gave me flashbacks of Bumper holding one to his lips and trying to get his asthma medicine inside of his lungs.

What was Doc Westin doing with all of these inhalers?

There was a big brown paper bag folded at the top. I took it out and sat it to the side.

Underneath the inhalers and a prescription pad was one of those old-time diaries that young girls used to have. I clicked in on the snap to open it, it was locked. I shook my head. The lock was easily picked, and it was funny that he thought it could hold his secrets from anyone who wanted to know what they were.

Like me.

I opened the desk draw and retrieved a letter opener and jimmied the lock. Once the pages were free to be searched, I turned to the first page. The heading was: Alternative Cancer Treatments. The next line read: Cancer type: non-Hodgkin lymphoma. Five Year Survival Rate: 70%.

I guess he did have cancer.

I flipped through the book. He had different sections labeled: Food. Exercise. Herbs. I started with herbs. After all, plant information was what I was after.

He had three columns, every line filled, some were starred. Only a few I recognized: *HuaChanSu, milk thistle, amygdalin, curcumin, ricin*.

I stopped reading. There it was. Ricin. It was one of the entries that was starred. I don't know why I thought it wouldn't be there, Auntie had told me that he'd considered using it to help cure his cancer. Who knows, he might have even tried it.

I sat the diary aside and moved stuff around in the box. No Bumper file. No mention of him anywhere. Still, in that box was everything that had been used to kill Bumper. I didn't have to look any further. I'd found the murder weapon.

Now what was I supposed to do with this information?

I moved my hand to bring it up to hold my head, it felt heavy, but accidently knocked the brown bag I'd set on the desk onto the floor.

What's in here?

I opened it up and found little blue, plastic containers with white tops. There were a couple dozen or more. I picked one up. Written on a piece of masking tape attached to the lid was B17.

B17. I knew that. It was associated with amygdalin.

Ahhh... I had seen that on his list of alternative treatment. I opened it up and there were seeds inside. I picked up several other blue containers out of the bag and they had labels that matched the names of things from Doc Westin's list for alternative cancer treatments.

Did he have one for ricin?

I dug through the bag and found it. It was empty.

"What happened to you?" I said, speaking out loud as I looked into the empty container. "Did Doc Westin use you, or did someone else take you?"

I let out a breath I hadn't even realized I was holding and thought about what I should do.

Tell my cousin, the sheriff? Even though I'd told Pogue what killed Bumper, I was sure that Pogue hadn't discovered yet that the killer had easy access to the murder weapon thanks to the lady Voodoo herbalists who were growing castor beans in their backyards. And I surely didn't want to tell him it was because of Auntie Zanne it was being grown.

I could just imagine how that would go. He'd want to question her and she wouldn't cooperate. It would be a rehash of what had happened in the first murder investigation. She'd been so awful to him, smacking him with her wooden spoon for questioning Josephine Gail, keeping information from him, and generally telling him that he didn't have what it took to figure a murder out. And in the end, when she and I were the ones who figured it out, it didn't do much for his ego. Although it wasn't entirely his fault, he did have to go out of town leaving us there to snoop.

Was there some way I could tell him about what I'd found and not tell him the part that Auntie Zanne had played?

Wait...

I cocked my head to the side and frowned. What was I even considering telling him? I thought about my conclusions, it was even more outlandish than Auntie Zanne's gratuity and bribery murder plot.

My theory, if you looked between the lines, was that Doc Westin, the man with the inhalers and missing ricin, was the person who had killed Bumper Hackett, even though he'd been dead a good two months before it happened. I'd come to that decision because he was the only one who had both of the instruments of his death.

Geesh, maybe I really should just leave the investigating up to Pogue, because that sounded crazy..

Chapter Thirty-One

"Why would you even tell them to meet you at Angel's Grace?" I asked.

"I thought Rhett and Hailey were going to be there."

We were on our way to the Community Center. Auntie hadn't said two words about bribery and murder to Shane Blanchard and Coach Buddy when she'd seen them at the funeral yesterday, or so I thought. But after we got home, Auntie had sprung it on me that after I had excused myself from their conversation, she'd asked them to come and meet her at the Community Center the next morning.

"And where are they now?" I said, not sure I wanted to know the answer. "Are they coming?"

"I don't know," she said, "I couldn't reach either one of them."

"Are they together?"

"Who?"

"Rhett and Hailey," I said.

Auntie Zanne sucked her tongue. "Why do you want to know that?"

"Never mind," I said.

"What if they bring some more of the poison?"

"Who?" My turn to ask.

"Shane Blanchard and Coach Buddy."

"And what poison would that be?"

"The poison they used to kill Bumper," she said.

"Oh my," I said. "What exactly did you tell them when you

arranged for them to meet you?"

"That I needed to talk to them about one of the football players."

"That sounds innocent enough," I said.

"They might have read between the lines."

"And what did it say 'between the lines'?"

"That I knew they were killers."

"Just don't go," I said. "If you're that afraid of them."

Auntie was driving the car. If it had been me, I would have just turned around and gone home, she wouldn't have had a choice.

"I'm not afraid."

"Then why are you shaking like a leaf on a tree?"

She held out a hand and looked at it. "I'm cold," she said.

"It's nearly seventy degrees."

"I'm anemic," she said.

"You're scared," I said. "But there is no need to be. No need to be afraid of them. No need to meet them. I don't think they did anything."

"Well, I do. I think they killed Bumper and I need to question both of them. I wish LaJay was coming too."

"You want to add more people? Why? You're not scared enough?"

"I told you I'm not scared."

"Okay."

"I just want to talk to him."

"And ask him did they pay him to go to A&M and in return he'd kill his lifelong friend, Bumper?"

"Exactly."

"Yeah, I'd be scared too if I were you."

"It's nervous energy," she said.

"Make up your mind," I said. "And tell me this, what are you going to do when they all confess?"

"I don't know now."

"You don't know?"

"I told you, I thought Rhett was going to be there. I can always reach him. Heck, it can be two o'clock in the morning and he answers. I don't know what he's doing now that he doesn't pick up."

I wished she'd stop implying Rhett was somehow wrapped up with that woman, Hailey Aaron, because I knew that's exactly what she wanted me to think that was what she thought. And really, the thought of it did make my heart go all aflutter. I was going to need a defibrillator to get it back on track.

I sucked my tongue. *Why was I even worried about Rhett and that woman?*

"Auntie," I said, shaking my head clear of Rhett thoughts, "just use my cellphone. Call Shane or that coach guy, and tell them you'll meet with them at another time."

"Do you want to solve this?" I think with her words, she pressed down harder on the accelerator, "or not?"

I braced myself against the dashboard. "We're not going to solve Bumper's murder by questioning these guys, that's for sure. Because they didn't do it." I glanced over at her. "You want to slow down?"

"You want to stop thinking that those two aren't coldblooded killers?"

"I could perhaps understand LaJay doing it," I said, trying to reason with her, "to get the girl, but not all three of them."

"Well, it's too late now, we're here and there they are." She swung into the parking lot, hitting the apron of the parking lot so fast that it nearly made me bump my head on the top of the car. "Already here. Lying in wait," she said.

"What are you going to ask them?" I said.

"Just thought I'd wing it," she said, pushing the gear into park. "And I didn't think I'd have to wing it for long. I figured the Cavalry would roll in and this case would be closed."

"Chase lied to me about the inhaler," I said, maybe updating her on the information I had would deter her from questioning these two guys. "Maybe it was him that killed Bumper." I nodded, wanting her to agree with me.

"How did he lie?"

"He told me that he hadn't seen Bumper's inhaler."

"That *was* a lie."

"How do you know that that's a lie?" I asked, scrutinizing her.

"I have my ways," she said.

"Piper told me yesterday at the funeral that he had it," I said, wondering how she knew. "They were in the front yard that day talking. I believe her."

"Miriam Colter told me that he had it."

"The organist?" I asked.

"Yep."

"Is that what you were going to tell me at the funeral?"

"I don't know," she said. "I can't think right now. I've got to concentrate on interrogating these two." She hitched a thumb in Shane Blanchard and Coach Buddy's direction. "I'm going to talk to them. You give Rhett one more call and see if he and his partner, Special Agent Aaron can't get here."

"Is that what she is?" I asked. "A special agent?"

"I'm telling you they only put the most qualified in charge of things like this. Top level."

"And what exactly do you want me to tell them when I reach Rhett?"

"Tell 'em to come guns a-blazin'."

"Why were you two at Bumper's funeral?" Auntie was saying when I walked in the door. I had gotten ahold of Rhett, who wanted me to spend time explaining why Auntie thought he was running a sting operation. It's what happens when you give Babet Derbinay a tiny piece of information, I had told him. She inflates it like a soufflé.

He'd told Auntie he had some affiliation with the FBI and that was all it took. Seemed like he should have known better than to tell her something like that.

"Why were you there?" Auntie Zanne was saying, her small five-foot-three frame standing in front of their towering, six-foot or more ones. Wagging a finger at them, she didn't act frightened in the least little bit.

Where had she gotten all that courage from in the last three minutes? I stood back and watched her in action.

"We wanted to show our respect," Shane said, his brow creased in confusion.

"Or was it that you wanted to announce your authority?" she said.

"What does that mean?" Coach Buddy said.

"Was that payback for Bumper not going to Texas A&M?" Auntie asked.

"Not coming to A&M?" the assistant coach said. "What'dya mean? You talking about two years ago?"

"Was what payback?" Shane said. He looked at the coach and back at Auntie. It was plain to see, they didn't know what she was talking about.

"His death. Or should I say murder?"

"Oh." Coach Buddy said the word and left his mouth in the shape it formed when it came out.

Shane Blanchard was quiet for a moment, brows knitted together, until it hit him what Auntie Zanne was saying. "Are you accusing me of murder?" Shane blurted out the words.

"Maybe both of you," she said.

"That's laughable," Shane Blanchard said.

"I'm not laughing," Auntie said, and put both of her hands on her hips.

Just then the door swung open and I thought, *Thank God, Rhett is here. I won't have to be the one to intervene.*

But as I turned I saw it was a troupe of old people coming in, it seemed, to rally her.

"Babet!?" Chester came charging in the door first. "What's going on? Are you okay?"

A stream of white hair, hunched shoulders and wide-eyed people, swinging cloth bags, canes and purses filed in, all gravitating behind Auntie Zanne forming a wedge, seemingly a tactical formation as they prepared for war.

I chuckled. I had no doubt, with the looks on their faces, they could take down the two men opposing Auntie Zanne. I recognized Senior-Would-Be-Soldier Chester. He was a Roble Belle, but none of the others were. I scanned their ranks, and I saw Miriam Coulter. The organist. Ahh... These must be the JOY Club members.

"What are they doing to you?" one of them asked. This senior was a blast from the eighties—flowered leggings, a windbreaker, sun visor, tennis shoes, and a fanny pack.

"What are *we* doing to *her*?" Mighty Max exec Shane Blanchard boomed. "She's accusing us of murder."

"Who did they kill, Babet?" another one asked, stepping forward, holding her purse ready to strike. I wasn't sure if she'd hit anything. She had on thick glasses, her head tilted up, peering through the bottom of her lenses to make her focus better.

"Somebody call the police." I heard a voice cracked with age. "We'll hold them until they get here."

"I've got the FBI coming," Auntie Zanne said and looked my way. I nodded, acknowledging that I had reached Rhett.

"The FBI?" Coach Buddy finally found the ability to speak. "Why in the world would you call the FBI?"

"You know why," Auntie Zanne said. "It is illegal to run a bribery operation and then kill someone to hide it."

"What the heck!" The coach took off his baseball cap and ran his hand over his head. He did a complete one-eighty, shook his head then turned back to face the Senior Soldiers. "You've got to be kidding, right? Who did we kill?"

"Who did *you* kill, you mean," Shane said. "Because I didn't kill anyone."

The coach frowned. "I didn't either."

"Bumper Hackett," Auntie Zanne said. "That's who."

"*Bumper!... Not Bumper!... We need to get them! They messed with the wrong town!*" Came the cries from Auntie's warmongers, and I felt that it was time for me to step in.

"Okay," I said. I went over and stood between the two factions, facing Auntie's group. I held up my hand. "We are not vigilantes. If these men did do anything wrong," I swiveled around from the waist, looked at them, and turned back, "which we don't know for sure that they did," I narrowed my eyes at Auntie, "then we'll let the authorities take care of it."

"Don't be a traitor," Auntie Zanne said to me through clenched teeth.

"I'm not," I said. "I'm just trying to stop a riot, keeping all the Rodney Kings of the world safe." I heard the door open and glanced that way. "And here comes Rhett."

Rhett came in the door smiling. He knew about Auntie's shenanigans, although he swore he'd never known her to do anything harebrained. This time he'd have to admit that she was over the top. But if he was really in the middle of an undercover investigation, and she'd blown his cover now with her accusations, I wouldn't expect him to be so happy about it.

"Where's Hailey?" Auntie said, wanting every member of her perceived Delta Force to be ready and present. "She'll probably want to take part in this."

"I got this," Rhett said. "Hi Romaine," he said, looking over at me.

I waved at him.

"How about if you take this youth group into another room," he spoke to me with that stupid smile of his, "while I talk to Babet and her captives."

"Happily," I said. Anything to get away from Crazy-Lady-Zanne.

Chapter Thirty-Two

I led the way for the group into the day room. I felt as if I should be giving them milk and a piece of fruit, leading armchair exercises, or something with them.

"Did those guys kill Bumper?" one of the seniors asked, she was sporting blue-dyed, fresh perm locks.

"I don't know," I said. "That's for the sheriff to find out."

"I thought the FBI was going to work on it?" Miriam Colter said.

I glanced back toward the front room and saw Rhett having a calm conversation with Auntie Zanne, Coach Buddy and Shane. I'd have to ask him what secret he had to get Auntie to unruffle.

I didn't know if Rhett was FBI, and if he were, if anyone was supposed to know it, I formed my answer with that in mind. "Bumper's murder," I said to the group, "from the information I know right now, is a local matter."

"What do you know?" a particularly unhappy-looking senior asked. She kept her eyes on Auntie and was breathing heavily. I didn't know if it was because she was upset about what was going on in the other room, or because she had trouble breathing due to a medical condition.

"She knows because she's a doctor," Chester said.

"You're a doctor?" Unhappy Senior said, nothing in her tone or words said she believed that. Her eyes stayed on Auntie Zanne.

I moved to stand in her line of view. I didn't want whatever was happening in the other room to incite her ire any further. "I am a doctor. A medical examiner just like Doc Westin was."

"Are you going to be our doctor now?" the only other gentleman in the group asked. He wore his plaid pants high up on his waist, securing them with a belt that was pulled past its last notch and a yellow golf shirt tucked in tight.

"No," I said and smiled. "I don't think so."

"Because we need one," Fanny-Pack-Lady said. "Someone to take Doc Westin's place and help us."

"I took his place in the JOY Club," Chester said. "Since they were short one member. You know, after the Doc passed."

"You couldn't take his place," the Unhappy Senior said. "He was one of a kind. He was good to us. Took care of us."

"He didn't take all that good care of us." I looked at the speaker. It was Miriam Colter. I probably needed to speak to her. She'd been upfront at the wedding, and possibly told Auntie Zanne, although she conveniently couldn't remember, that she saw Chase pick up the inhaler Bumper had when he collapsed.

But now probably wasn't the best time. Plus, I was surprised at her words against Doc Westin and wanted to find out the difference the two of them had.

"Mrs. Colter," I said, "you're upset with Doc Westin?"

"Upset doesn't even start to describe what I am with that man," she said, I remembered that shaky voice from the stand-down earlier.

"What happened between the two of you?" I asked.

"He told me he was going to take care of a matter for me and he didn't."

"He died," another senior said, she was wearing a colorful muumuu. Her face and arms thick and rosy. "He would have taken care of it, but he couldn't."

"I don't believe it," Miriam said, pulling her purse up close to her thin chest and clutching it tightly. "He had plenty of time. Heck. It happened more than two years ago now. And I never got my money back. I don't $500 just to give away."

"You didn't have to send the money to them," Fanny-Pack-

Lady said.

Miriam Colter slammed her cane down and used it to push herself up, she leaned against it and raised her voice, at least I think she would consider it yelling. "I was tricked," she said, her voice straining to push more decibels out. "They tricked me. I wasn't the only one it happened to, so watch your mouth about what you say to me."

"What happened?" I asked. Then I remembered. There were the initials M.C. in Doc Westin's book.

That must be Miriam Colter.

It had said that she lost $500 in some sort of scam.

"I don't want to talk about it," she said and looked around the room.

I took another look at Rhett. If he were FBI, then a Medicare scam would be right up his alley. Maybe he could help. Plus, according to Doc Westin's note, one of my prime suspects in Bumper's murder, Chase Turner, was involved somehow, at least his name was written in the Doc's notebook

"Would you like to go somewhere else?" I wanted her to feel free to speak. "We can talk in private," I said.

"We've heard enough of her whining," Unhappy Senior said. "We came to check on the mums for homecoming."

"I think they're down the hall," I said. "In the last room there."

"We know where they are," she said with a huff. "We put them there."

They all filed out but Miriam Colter and the woman that sat next to her. "We can go into the office," I said, not knowing if she wanted more privacy. I looked at the other woman and smiled, not wanting her to feel put out. "I'm willing to listen to you and see what I can do to help."

"This is my friend, Judith Dorsch." Mrs. Colter pointed to the woman. "She was scammed, too."

The J.D. in Doc Westin's notes.

They were the only two people he mentioned specifically, although he had written that others were involved. She didn't seem as in much of a huff as Mrs. Colter. Her face filled with wrinkles, she wore ruby red lipstick which was spread outside of her natural lip line and had smeared onto her teeth.

"So what happened?" I said.

"I can't talk long," Miriam Colter said, she let her eyes trail behind the other seniors. "I'm in charge of the mums this year."

"Okay," I said. I didn't want to talk too much, let her do it so she wouldn't feel I wasn't really interested.

"I was scammed and I know who done it," she said.

"No she doesn't," she said. "We had an idea, and Doc Westin was looking into it."

"You had a name?" I asked.

"No." Mrs. Dorsch looked at Mrs. Colter. "We're sure it was a young person. A boy. Didn't sound past his twenties, the one that called me."

"Same here," Mrs. Colter said.

"It was more than just us two that were scammed," Mrs. Dorsch said. "And a couple of them said that the one that called them didn't sound that young. One even said it was a female voice."

"So it sounds like it was more than one person that was involved," I said.

"A ring," Mrs. Colter said.

"What exactly happened?" I asked, recalling the notes that Doc Westin had written.

"Someone called us," Mrs. Dorsch said.

"A young boy," Mrs. Colter interrupted. "No more than seventeen or eighteen."

Mrs. Dorsch nodded. "Told us that there was a new insurance for Medicare Part D. If we paid $500, we'd get our prescriptions for free from now on and no more co-pays for doctor visits."

"I spend that much in one month for co-pays and prescriptions," Miriam Colter said. "Sounded real good to me."

"But it turned out not to be good," Mrs. Dorsch said. "We gave them our credit card information, they processed it and we never heard from them again."

"A scam," Mrs. Colter said. "Who would scam old people?" She shook her head. "We're just trying to live out our last days in peace. Not bothering anyone."

"Scammers target the elderly," I said, "because they think they are easy prey."

"Easy prey, my butt." She bit her bottom lip and shook her head. "Well, you better believe, in this case," Mrs. Colter said, "the hunter is going to be captured by his game."

I raised my eyebrows. I didn't want to chuckle because this was very serious. But she acted as if she was ready to kill.

"Did you speak to the authorities?" I asked.

"I already told you," she said, "Doc Westin was supposed to do it. Promised me he'd take care of it. But he didn't."

"How many times we got to tell you," Mrs. Dorsch shifted in her seat to face her friend, "the man died. He couldn't do anything."

"It doesn't matter because I took care of it myself," she said. "They won't be doing it to nobody else."

Chapter Thirty-Three

Auntie was always up and into her shenanigans early.

By the time I left Angel's Grace it was just past noon. Plenty of day left, and I figured I'd do a little investigating of my own. I decided that I needed to go and see Mrs. Westin.

After going through his boxes, I wanted to know just what Doc Westin had been up to. I had shoved my thoughts about him somehow being involved in Bumper Hackett's murder down deep in the back of my brain. But if I was going to solve this murder, I figured I'd better find out why he wrote prescriptions for Bumper, and if it was possible that he had ricin stashed that someone could get their hands on.

I swung by the ME's office and picked up a couple of Doc Westin's personal boxes. I needed a pretense for going to see his wife. Auntie had done the funeral for the good doctor, but as usual, I stayed pretty much out of sight. I didn't want his wife thinking I was just coming by to be nosy, even though I was.

The Westin's lived in a ranch house in a rural community right outside of Roble. Long and low, their yellow house had green shutters around its large windows. A big porch was bordered by white spindles, a banister and two rocking chairs painted green sat on the gray wooden floor.

Mrs. Lillian Westin was in her late sixties, she was short and squat, with long hair that was still mostly black. She had it pulled back in a bun, tiny gold hoops adorned her ears, and the only other jewelry she wore was a wedding band.

"Hi Mrs. Westin," I said. She had answered the door in her house slippers, a screen door between us.

"Hi Romaine," she said.

"You remember me?" I said. "I hoped you would."

"Everyone knows Babet's girl, the doctor. She's not going to let anyone forget you. She's so proud of you."

"That's my auntie," I said. "I wanted to bring you some boxes Doc Westin left at his old office."

"Oh, thank you," she said and pushed open the screen. "Just set them right inside the door. I was just getting ready to come out and sit on the porch. Enjoy me a little fresh air. You want to sit with me?"

"Sure," I said. "That'll be nice."

"You want some sweet tea?" she asked.

"No thank you," I said. "I'm fine."

"I'm glad you brought by those boxes," she said stepping outside, "because otherwise you might not have stopped by and I might not have seen nary a hide of any living soul today. I get so lonely around here these days and I'll take any excuse to get some company.

"I'm happy to keep you company," I said.

We sat in the rockers, and Mrs. Westin started a slow steady rock.

"So, I hear that you are taking over Harley's practice."

That was gossip, sure enough, not the kind I was fishing for, and somehow I knew my Auntie Zanne had started it.

"No," I said. "County Commissioners offered it to me, but I'm going back to Chicago."

"Oh," she said. "When are you going back?"

Good question.

"I have to find a job first. The job I had downsized."

"Then why go back looking for one, if you have a job here?"

Sounded like she'd been talking to Auntie Zanne.

Or maybe, Romaine, that just makes sense...

"The new facility looks really nice," I said. "I think Doc Westin would have been pleased."

"I know he would've," she smiled, "he was always complaining about that old one. And besides me wanting you to keep me company, I appreciate you bringing me his things. I thought there must've not been anything worth keeping after I didn't hear from Miriam once she got the place packed up."

"The new office inherited everything that was left," I said. "When they finished the new place, I had all the things from the old office moved to the new one."

"I see," she said and nodded. "I just figured that there wasn't anything personal he'd left."

"Did you say Miriam before?" I asked, my mind just catching up with my ears. "Do you mean Miriam Colter?"

"Yes. She helped Harley out sometimes. A nurse of sorts." She nodded a confirmation. "Mostly with the seniors, and then down at the office." She chuckled. "Not with autopsies or anything like that. Harley did those all by himself."

"Oh that was nice of Mrs. Colter," I said to Mrs. Westin, but to myself I said, "What?" I couldn't believe my ears. I cleared my throat. "So, Miriam Colter packed up Dr. Westin's office?"

"I already told you that, dear." She looked at me. "Can you hear me okay?"

"Yes, ma'am," I said. I had heard her loud and clear, I was just distracted because I knew what was in those boxes and now I knew it had been Miriam Colter who had put it there. "I just saw Mrs. Colter today."

"You did?" she asked.

"Yes, she was with the JOY Club at Angel's Grace. They were working on mums for homecoming."

"Homecoming," Mrs. Westin said. "This'll be the first year I'll miss it. Harley and I would go every year. He loved football you know. He didn't care if it was high school, college or professional."

"I haven't been to a football game since I can't remember when."

"Oh, I enjoy them," she said. "Harley's favorite season." She smiled at the memory. "And Harley loved to rub elbows with the players. Every year he'd have the varsity over for a bar-b-que."

"Roble's varsity team?" I asked.

"Do you need to sit closer to me?" she asked. "So you can hear?"

Auntie Zanne was always asking me if I had cotton in my ears. It wasn't that I couldn't hear, it was that I surprised at what she was saying and I wanted to make sure I got it right.

"No ma'am," I said. "I can hear you just fine. I was just surprised that Doc Westin invited the high school team over."

"Why?" she said and looked at me.

It was true, I didn't know much about him so how could something he did surprise me? I didn't know what was usual for him and what wasn't.

"I don't know," I said and shrugged, trying to make up for my uninformed response. "You know how sometimes young people don't like to hang out with people who are much older."

"Oh, they loved Harley. Lots of times they'd come to him for medical help."

That made my ears perk up. Had Bumper come to him for medical help? Help possibly with his asthma? That was the kind of information I was fishing for. "I thought Doc Westin was just the medical examiner," I said.

"Oh no. He was a lot more to so many people around here."

"Yes. I see that he was." I bit my lip, not sure how to ask the next question, so I just spat it out. "Did Doc Westin ever treat Michael Hackett?"

"Bumper?"

Oh, so she knew him...

"Yes," I said.

"Yep," she said and smiled. "He was the doctor, confidant, and member to the JOY Club. He was their sometime doctor and an all-time fan of the local football team. So many things to so many people." I saw her smile fade, and a mistiness cover her eyes. I didn't want her to start crying, I still hadn't found out if it was possible that Doc Westin did give Bumper inhalers. Possibly ones laced with ricin for God knows what reason. Tears would stall if not stop my questioning. And, I hadn't found out anything about his alternative cancer treatments, the reason he needed the ricin in the first place. How was I going to bring up his cancer, when just the subject of football brought on tears?

"When I first wanted to become a doctor," I said, getting ready to not tell a whole truth, "Dr. Westin really helped me."

"He did?" she said and smiled, sniffing back the urge her eyes had to tear. "See. Like I said, he liked helping people. I couldn't picture him as anything else but a doctor."

"So did he help Bumper with his asthma?" I asked, not wanting her to get too distracted.

"Mostly it was Delores he helped."

"Mrs. Hackett? How so?"

"She was frantic over Bumper playing ball and having asthma, only Harley told me he'd mostly grown out of it. Hadn't had an episode in a while and knew his triggers," she looked at me, "at least that's what Harley called them."

"That's what they're called," I said and nodded.

"Harley told me that even Bumper's pediatrician wouldn't write prescriptions for inhalers anymore. Said Bumper was nigh grown and his adult doctor should check him out to see if he still needed it."

"Looked like he needed them the day he died," I said.

"Must have done something to trigger it then."

"I guess so," I said.

I knew that people outgrew asthma. I also remembered hearing that he hadn't had an episode in a couple of years. What made him have one the day of the ceremony?

Mrs. Westin yawned and I knew I wouldn't have her full attention much longer, especially with all my questions, even if she was happy to have company. I moved on to my next topic.

"And when I went through the boxes to see if anything was personal that you might like," I smiled sweetly, "I saw where Doc

Westin been doing research on alternative treatments. It was fascinating, and as a medical professional I was really interested in it. I hope it's okay that I held on to the box."

"The alternative cancer treatments?"

"Yes ma'am."

"Yes." She nodded slowly and took a minute to speak. "He had cancer." She looked at me. "Many people didn't know that."

"I wouldn't tell anyone anything we discuss," I said. "I've taken an oath."

"Hippocratic Oath," she said, nodding, "it says you've got to have medical confidentiality."

"Yes ma'am," I said. "It does."

"Harley warned me about that almost every time he came home and told me about a patient. And believe me, I never repeated anything he said about a case. Except for the dead ones. Harley said those were public knowledge."

"The research had a lot to do with natural methods of treating cancer," I said, "likes herbs and roots. That's why I found it so interesting because you know, I grew up around that."

"Most people think of Babet as a doctor in her own right," Mrs. Westin said. "With her herbs and teas. They've helped a lot of people around here. When Harley first got his diagnosis, he went straight to Babet."

"He did?" I said.

"Yes he did." She gave a single nod. "Wanted to learn what she knew about so he could treat his cancer. Then he tried growing his own garden." She chuckled. "That didn't work out too well."

"He couldn't grow anything?"

"Nothing!" she said. "I told him he should just stick to traditional medicine and let Babet do the gardening."

Chapter Thirty-Four

I got more information than I bargained for from Mrs. Westin. I felt bad using her for information, especially after she told me she was lonely and missing her husband. I suggested that perhaps she should join the JOY Club. Chester had said he took the last spot, but I'm sure they could find room to make for their favorite member's wife.

I had stayed a good hour with Mrs. Westin, and when I got ready to leave she made me promise I'd come back to see her. I got into the car and as soon as I drove off, my mind went into overdrive.

I had discovered that Miriam Colter had access to all the things it took to murder Bumper. She had packed up the boxes, making it easy for her to get what she needed. She came to the wedding and was close to Bumper.

But why would she leave her evidence behind packed in boxes? And how did she manage to get Bumper to take the inhaler she'd rigged? Could she have even thought and carried out such a devious plan?

Auntie Zanne did say she was mean and sneaky, and Miriam herself had said that she'd taken care of whoever had wronged her. Would that include committing murder? Did she think Bumper was the young voice that had wronged her? And would her killing scheme have Doc Westin in it? Did she take care of him, too, because he failed to do what he had promised?

I wasn't sure, although it almost sounded as far-fetched as

Auntie's assessment of who the murderers were.

I needed to figure this out.

I couldn't go and discuss it with Auntie, she was at one of her many meetings. Planning the homecoming dinner. Her life was so full of things to do. She always tried to get me to go with her, and I'd fight going, digging my claws deep to keep her from dragging me along. But for some reason, at this moment, I couldn't say why I never wanted to go.

I pulled up to a stop light and put my foot on the brake. I blew out a breath and laid my head on the steering wheel. I had to take that back. I did know why I started thinking about it.

I was lonely, too.

And talking to Mrs. Westin had made me realize it. Right now I needed someone to talk to and the only person I had was Auntie Zanne and she was busy. Sure, she'd say she was never too busy for me, but she had a million things to do.

And she was right, I didn't have any friends.

What a thing to figure out.

The light turned green and I pressed down on the accelerator. I felt tears well up in my eyes, but then I realized how stupid it would be to cry. I was always talking about my carefully crafted life. I had done this to myself. And there was no reason to cry, it was what I had wanted.

What I thought I had wanted.

There was no one now I could call or drop by to see. And all I wanted to do was get back to Chicago because I thought my friends were there. I shook my head. I hadn't heard from one of them.

I tried to put my mind back on the murder. The autopsy. The investigation. All those things fulfilled me. Trying to solve it with Auntie, going back and forth with my cousin, Pogue—that excited me.

It made me happy.

When I looked up, I realized that I was driving down the road to Catfish's place. I had come here on autopilot

How did I get here, I started to say, then I realized it was because I knew that Catfish was someone I could always count on to be there for me. He was another good thing in my life.

"Hi," he said, standing on the other side of the screen door, that bashful smile of his spread across his face.

"Auntie said I don't have any friends," I said.

"You've got me," he said and pushed open the door. "Always have. Always will."

"Thank you," I said and stepped inside the house.

"I was just on my way out to the dock," he said, walking toward the back. "Sit a while and think. Maybe cast a line."

"Sounds good," I said and followed him.

Catfish had acres of land, passed down through generations, part of the land his family got in their grant in the mid-1800s of "forty acres and a mule." His family had been lucky. Most of the land allocated during the war ex-slaves under agrarian reform wasn't allowed to keep it. The land got restored to pre-war owners. Not theirs.

I took off my shoes, rolled up my pant legs and sat on the dock, dangling my toes in the water.

Catfish sat in a chair and picked up his fishing pole. "You know I got a chair up here for you."

"I know," I said. "But I like sitting here."

"Nice day."

"Yeah. It is a nice day."

We sat quietly for a while. Basking in the warm October day, not needing any words between us to enjoy each other's company.

"You figured who killed Bumper yet?"

"Well, that just came out the blue," I said and chuckled. "What makes you think I'm trying to figure that out?"

"You figured out the last one," he said. "I remember you like a good puzzle. Plus, I figured you wouldn't let Babet take charge of a murder investigation as a justice of the peace. She'd get it into a tangled mess."

I laughed. "I think she already has."

"Yeah? How so."

"She's got one college's assistant football coach, a Mighty Max marketing exec, and one of Bumper's childhood friends committing the murder."

"Wow," he said. A word he liked to use. "That's pretty out there."

"Not as out there as a couple of theories I've been mulling over."

"Oh yeah? What you got?"

"My murder suspects include a man who has been dead for two months and an eighty-year old woman who can hardly hold herself upright."

"Oh wow," he said. "You're getting to be just as bad as your Auntie Zanne."

Chapter Thirty-Five

It was nearly four thirty when I left Catfish's place. I was hungry and tired, but I had one more stop to make before I headed home.

"Hey, Cousin," I said as I walked inside of the Sheriff's Office. I needed to drop off the toxicology report to Pogue, and maybe share notes with him on the murder investigation so far. I couldn't let him know too much of what I was doing because he'd told me not to do anything.

He was standing at a table that had a coffee machine, cups and a box of donuts on it.

"Hi," he said, happy to see me. "What you doing here?"

"Can't I stop in to see my cousin?"

"Romie, you know you're not one for visiting," he said.

"Why does everyone think I'm so antisocial?"

"Uh, because you are."

I waved the envelope at him. "I brought you a present."

"Ahh," he said. "Now I see why you're here."

"One day I'm going to surprise you and just stop by to say, hi."

He laughed. "I look forward to that day."

"I thought you'd be on your way out, not still working." I glanced up at the clock on the wall.

"I'm busy, what can I say."

"Who knew there was so much crime in Roble," I said, almost facetiously, although things were a-changing.

"Yeah, all this murder business is something."

"The crime I'm talking about was some kind of Medicare Part

D scam I just found out about earlier. Someone perpetrating it on the seniors around here."

"You've been talking to Miriam Colter."

"Yeah," I said and raised an eyebrow. "She said something to you about it?"

"Oh my, that's all I can hear from her." He shook his head. "She wants me to go and arrest every person in town under eighteen."

"Oh," I said, "because the voice sounded young that made the call to her house?"

"Right and when it first happened that might have made sense. But that was two years ago. It's possible that by now they'd be an adult."

I laughed. "You weren't even sheriff two years ago."

"I know, but when I got elected she thought she had a new ear to bend about it. Somebody she hoped who would open up an investigation."

"Are you going to look into it?" I asked.

"The other sheriff did some preliminary work on it, I guess. He looked into some juvie records, found out who were some of the little hooligans at the time who might be involved in it or maybe knew about it."

"Didn't find anything?"

"No. But that might be interesting to you, Michael Hackett was one of the juvie records he pulled."

"Bumper?"

"Yeah, seems like he and a couple of his friends liked to cause a little havoc back then. Got into a little trouble."

"They're all in college now," I said. "Well, Bumper was in college. And his friends are—the ones I met that is."

"Yeah, one of them had been into some trouble for credit card theft. But what I've learned from the last sheriff's investigation, if you want to call it that, there was no way a bunch of high school pranksters could have pulled it off. Someone older, more experienced had to have been running that scam."

"Maybe they employed teenagers?" I asked. "That's why the seniors thought the voices were of young people?"

"Seniors?" he asked. "Who else?"

"I was at Angel's Grace when I heard about it. Seniors from the JOY Club told me about it."

"Oh," he said and slowly nodded. "No one has come to me but Miriam Coulter. She's probably filling their heads with it." He huffed. "Hope it won't make more work for me."

"Why didn't you tell Mrs. Coulter that the FBI would have to be in charge of a federal scam like that?"

"Do you think that would have stopped her from bugging me about it? No. Said she couldn't get to 'no FBI office'."

"Well Auntie might have fixed that for her, she announced today in front of all of her seniors that Rhett was FBI."

"Good," Pogue said. "Maybe he can take some of the heat off of me. With this murder, I'm up to my ears in real police work. I don't have time for her imaginary crimes."

"I don't think it was imaginary," I said. "A lot of seniors lost money on that."

"You're not snooping around on this now, are you? What have you been doing?"

"Nothing," I said. He narrowed his eyes. "I haven't. They told me about it. Plus, Doc Westin had some personal items he left at the old office. I went through them to see if I should take them to his widow and I saw it mentioned."

"You found something about a Medicare scam?" he asked.

"Yeah. Doc Westin was trying to look into it for them."

"Where is the box?" he said. "Why didn't you bring it to me?"

"I'd thought I'd give the stuff to Rhett. You know, like we just discussed that would be the FBI's jurisdiction."

Time to get to what I really wanted information on.

"So... How is your murder investigation going?" I asked.

"No offense, Cousin, but that's none of your business."

*   *   *

Pogue's comment lit a fire under me.

I'm sure I reminded him of Auntie Zanne as I huffed and puffed my way out of there. I couldn't get to the car fast enough.

I didn't know what Pogue had, but between Auntie Zanne and me, I was sure I was ahead of him in the investigation game. We'd run a pretty comprehensive probe so far. Us catching the killer shouldn't be that far off, and I'd be willing bet that he didn't have the information we did.

And since he had an attitude, he wouldn't be getting any of my information.

I threw the car into drive, my tires screeching as I swerved into a U-turn. I glanced in my review mirror, in my mind daring him to come out of his office and just try and give me a ticket.

Auntie and I had spoken to all of our suspects—Auntie's had been Shane Blanchard and Coach Harold "Buddy" Budson. Initially mine were Bonnie Alvarez, Piper Alvarez and Chase Turner. I'd since added Doc Westin and Miriam Colter to my list. And so far, I hadn't been able to scratch any of them off.

Yes. Yes. Doc Westin died long before Bumper had, but it didn't mean he hadn't somehow set the wheels in motion and the murder wasn't carried out until later. Like lacing some of those inhalers with the deadly poison before giving them to Mrs. Hackett. Doc Westin hadn't any idea he'd die before his murder plot was played out, if indeed that was what happened.

Auntie's list was a whole different story. A bribery and gratuity operation, paying Roble football players to attend certain universities, or do endorsements for the popular Mighty Max sports drink once they hit the NFL. In my opinion her suspects, although she hadn't let go of the idea, probably had nothing to do with the murder. Still, her interrogation of them, if that's what you want to call it, was what led me to my fifth suspect. Doc Westin. In the end, for me, her suspects ended up having some useful purpose.

In my investigation, I'd discovered that Jorianne hadn't gotten

Bumper to the altar because of a threat with a deadly weapon, it was because she was the girl of his dreams. And I learned that not everyone wanted that union to take place, and some might have even been jealous of it. All motives for murder.

And then there was that best man who came out of nowhere and lied to me about the inhaler for no reason. Chase Turner. It seemed I couldn't get his full story from anyone.

Finally, I'd located a possible source for what was used as a murder weapon. Actually I had found the "gun and the bullet", as it were. A stash of inhalers and an empty container marked ricin. I pulled up to a stop sign, drumming my fingers on the steering wheel, I thought about our reconnaissance activities.

Yep. Auntie and I had been able to ask a lot of questions, make accusations and watch their reactions. I just needed to start putting the pieces together that I'd gathered.

Although, I still needed to find out what happened to the ricin that was missing from the empty container in Doc Westin's personal things. I wasn't sure any had ever been there, but I had to believe that it had possibly been there at one time. It just seemed to me that it would be easier for someone to get the protein already extracted than to get the castor bean and try to do it themselves, especially after Auntie told me how technically difficult it was to purify. And that was maybe what Doc Westin had because it was the only way it would've been any use to him as an alternative treatment for cancer.

So far, I figured it could be possible that Doc Westin, before he died, laced the inhalers with ricin. I didn't know why, sure it was improbable, he was a healer by profession, but it was possible. And now, thanks to Mrs. Westin, I'd learned that Miriam Coulter had access to the things Doc Westin had stashed as well. She was a more likely culprit because she was still alive. I thought about her and that cane—was there anyone else that could have been in those boxes? And if there was no one else... I shook my head.

I needed more information.

The driver of the car behind me laid on his horn. I guessed I'd stayed a little longer than necessary at the stop sign. I held up a hand that could be seen through the back window and waved my apologies. I pulled off, still lost in thought.

And at what point was I going to tell Pogue what I had found out? Being mad at him shouldn't stop me from divulging the information I had, even if it was sketchy. I knew that. It's true, he could test the container Doc Westin had marked ricin and find out if any had actually ever been in it. He could also dust it for fingerprints. But I just wasn't sure and I didn't want to send Pogue off on a wild goose chase. Right now I was running after my own tail, chasing ghosts and little old ladies. He didn't want me investigating anyway, and if I came to him with a half-cocked idea, Pogue would be even more upset with me.

It was possible that Doc Westin never did actually get any ricin out of one of the caster bean plants Auntie's herbalists grew, and that little plastic container had always been empty. Why get Pogue involved in that?

And if that were true, I'd have to look for another source.

Yep. For now, I'd keep quiet to Pogue about it until I had something more concrete. And for right now, I thought, it probably would be best to follow the Doc Westin lead—even if it meant a little old lady had to go to jail. I guess you just shouldn't mess with people's Medicare.

So where to start?

Doc Westin either had ricin or was trying to get it. Auntie Zanne had told me that. And I had to assume Auntie wasn't the one who had gotten ricin extracted because she told me she'd suggested Doc Westin not try to use it. That meant, if he did get it, he'd gone to another herbalist.

Auntie had given me four names. I only remembered two. Mark and Leonard Wilson.

Chapter Thirty-Six

The twins lived in a small cape cod down the road from our house. It was painted white with canary blue shutters, planter boxes underneath the mullioned windows were filled with an assortment of colorful flowers. There was a white picket fence and little stone gnomes and animals in the yard.

It had been too late to visit the sisters after I'd left Pogue's office. I knew the sisters got up and went to bed with the chickens. I couldn't let my Auntie Zanne know what I was up to. She'd be upset that I was questioning her friends about something she hadn't shared with them.

It was so hard to get out of the house, Auntie Zanne kept an eye out for me like a hawk. When I was working on the new ME facility, I had a reason to leave in the mornings and she never questioned me. But now with it all finished she had my days planned and couldn't understand why I didn't have time for whatever she wanted me to do.

"Where are you going?" she said. She walked out of one of the chapels while I was going out the front door. I just knew she'd be in the kitchen, where she was every morning this early. Oh, but not today.

"Out for a walk," I said. It wasn't a complete lie. I did plan on walking the quarter of a mile to the Wilson house.

"I've got things for you to help me with," she said. "Homecoming is in a couple of days and with all the stuff that's been going on since last Saturday's almost—wedding—"

"I can help you when I get back," I said, not letting her even start on her list of my to-dos.

She turned and looked at me, narrowing her eyes. "What are you up to, Romaine?" she said.

"I'm not up to anything," I said.

"Oh yeah you are." She circled around me looking at me up and down. "Did Alex call?"

"No."

"Is he meeting you outside?"

"No." She stood and stared at me. "Why do you think I'm up to something?" I asked.

"Because you never agree to help me that quickly. I usually have to threaten you."

"You never have to threaten me," I said.

"I'm watching you," she said, and made her fingers in a V, pointing at her eyes then back at me.

"Oh geesh!" I said. "I'll be back."

I walked out the house and started to go the opposite way of Mark and Leonard's house just to throw Auntie Zanne off. Then I thought, *how ridiculous. As old as I am, I'm hiding out from my auntie.*

There was no sidewalk along our county thoroughfare, Grand River Road, so I walked out into the street and headed toward the Wilson's place. I walked up to the door and knocked. No answer. I didn't think they'd be gone this early so I walked around to the back of the house.

Their backyard was as large as Auntie's even though their house was one tenth the size. Flowers were everywhere, leaving only a narrow stone walkway to get to their greenhouse.

"Morning," I called out as I approached.

I saw one of them wave me in. They were all smiles as I stepped inside. "Good morning," I said again.

"Good morning, Romaine," they said together.

"What do we owe this nice surprise to?" one said.

"You haven't been over to see us since you were a teenager," the other one said.

"Has it been that long?" I asked.

"Maybe longer." They spoke in unison.

"Well, that's just not right," I said. "I'll have to come and visit more often."

It was hard to tell the two apart, nowadays I used the pattern of the wrinkles on their faces, a sign of their seventy plus years to aid in their identification—Leonard's crow's feet were etched deeper and were longer than Mark's. but they didn't make telling them apart easy, as usual they were both dressed in the same plaid shift dress and matching green garden jackets. They had on beige stockings and green canvas tennis shoes.

"That would nice," Leonard said.

"But today, I came by to ask you a question, see if I couldn't get your help."

"We'll be happy to help you, won't we, Sister?"

"Of course, anything for you, Romaine."

"It's about your garden."

"Our garden?"

"Yes. I know that Auntie Zanne asked you to grow castor beans."

"How do you know that?" Leonard asked.

"It was supposed to be a secret," Mark added. "We didn't know why, but of course if Babet asked us to keep quiet about it, we wouldn't question it."

"She told me," I said, trying to convince them to talk to me, although if Auntie Zanne knew, she wouldn't approve of them breaking the confidence. And I didn't know if they'd taken some kind of Voodoo herbalist oath. "I'm helping solve Bumper's murder."

"Yes, Babet told us you both were working on it," Mark said. "What is it you'd like to know?"

She seemed more willing to talk, so I turned to her.

"I'm not sure if you know, Mark, that it was Doc Westin who was interested in it the castor bean," I said.

They looked at each other.

"We knew," Mark said.

"Doc Westin came to us," Leonard said.

"For us to help him," Mark said.

"He went behind Auntie Zanne's back?" I asked.

"Oh no," Leonard said.

"That's not what he was trying to do," Mark said.

"Babet was out of town," one twin said.

"Visiting you," the other one said.

"And because he couldn't get to her, he tried us. I don't know why he needed to have it so quickly."

"I thought that he didn't know who Auntie Zanne had growing it for him."

"He didn't," they said at the same time.

"But he knew that we knew about herbs," Leonard said.

"He knew that we were in the Ladies' Society with Babet," Mark said, finishing the explanation.

"The Ladies Society of Voodoo Herbalist," Leonard said.

"Yes," Mark said and nodded.

I loved the sisters dearly, but it was only so much I could take of them finishing each other's sentences and thoughts and then speaking at the same time. It was like being in an echo chamber. I needed to ask as few questions as possible to get to what I needed to know.

"Do you know why he wanted it?" I asked. "What he needed it for?"

"He told us," Leonard said.

"He wanted the ricin," Mark said.

"So did you give him any?"

They hung their heads. "No," they said, and nothing else. It felt, though, as if they weren't telling me something.

"If he seemed really interested in getting some, I'm thinking that he didn't stop with you two." I looked at them, and eyes wide they looked back. "But he might not have known who the other herbalists were."

"He didn't know," Mark said.

Leonard shook her head, and Mark started shaking hers in sync with her sister.

"Okay," I said. "Did you tell him?" I asked.

"We may have," Leonard said.

"And if we had," Mark said. "We would have told him that Delphine Griffith had actually extracted ricin even though Babet thought it was too hard to do."

Chapter Thirty-Seven

I had the name of one of the other herbalists that had grown castor beans. One of the women that Auntie had told me about—the one who lived in Shelby County.

Shelby was one of the three counties in our "tri-county" area. But where I needed to go was about a forty-five-minute drive. I glanced down at my fuel gauge. I needed gas.

Auntie always kept her vehicles on full. Never know when the funeral home had to make a run. It wouldn't be professional to have to stop and get gas when a grieving family was waiting. I had been borrowing her car all week and hadn't stopped to fill up once.

I drove about fifteen minutes on Highway 87 before I pulled off on an exit ramp to fill up.

I paid with my own credit card at the pump, figured I shouldn't expense the gas to the funeral home since I'd been doing all the driving. As I stood at the pump, I noticed a young girl walking my way, a smile on her face.

"Hi," she said. "Romaine, right?"

"Hi," I said, recognizing her. It was Gaylon, Mrs. Hackett's niece. "How are you?" I smiled back.

"I'm okay," she said. "You live out this way?" "Oh no," I said. "On my way to Shelby County to visit a friend of my auntie's."

She nodded. "On my way home," she said. "It's been a long week."

"Yes it has," I said, "but I'm sure it's been even a longer one for you."

"Yes it has been." She nodded. "My aunt has been so distraught. You know Bumper was her only child. She doted over him."

"Yes, I read that in the program at the funeral."

"But everyone has been so good to her. Neighbors from all over Roble, even Sabine County, coming over bringing food and helping out. Jorianne, her family and Bumper's friends from when he played for Roble High. They've all came and stood by her side."

"That is really nice," I said. "I'm sure she appreciates it."

"She does. But it still so hard for her to wrap her head around, you know?" Gaylon said.

"I can imagine," I said.

"Just think," Gaylon said, "last week his friends took him to Lake Charles for his bachelor's party. And this week we buried him."

"Lake Charles?" I said, confused. "I thought they went to Las Vegas. To the Golden Nugget."

"Oh no," she chuckled. "What? Did you see that picture on Facebook?"

"Yes, I did," I said, kind of embarrassed. "I don't have a Facebook account or anything, I just was just trying to get to know him better."

"Yeah. No. They went to the one in Lake Charles. Had it planned for weeks, and my Aunt Delores said Bumper was so excited." She smiled at the pleasant memory of her aunt. "They were trying to act as if it was Vegas, trying to make Bumper take the pictures down. You know: "What happens in Vegas, stays in Vegas. Apparently that counts for Lake Charles, too." She laughed. "They didn't get back until late Friday night. Jori was so upset, worried about him the whole time."

"Was he sick before he left?" I asked.

Her face went blank, her mouth opened. She titled her head to the side. "He wasn't sick at all, I thought," she said, her face twisted in confusion. "Wasn't that the conclusion that *you* came to? You said he'd been poisoned at the wedding."

Way to turn my words around on me, I thought. That finished her conversation with me after that. Her smile and pleasant demeanor disappeared and so did she. She walked off and got into her car and drove away without so much as a wave or backward glance.

Finished pumping the gas, I shook the nozzle and replaced it back onto the pump. I screwed in the cap and slammed the door to the gas compartment. I climbed into the car and blew out a breath.

I certainly hadn't meant to upset her. I was getting as bad as Auntie in trying to ask questions. I guess I should have phrased it better. She had no reason to know it had been a slow acting poison. Most times you're poisoned, you die, right then and there. And I'm sure Pogue hadn't released that information.

I slammed my hand on the steering wheel. I could have kicked myself for being so insensitive.

I checked my GPS and pulled off, my tires screeching behind me.

Chapter Thirty-Eight

Delphine Griffith looked like a bird. Round chest, long nose and spindly arms and fingers. Gray haired, she had gentle bright eyes. Round and blue. They reminded me of someone I knew, but I couldn't figure out who that could be.

"Good morning," she said.

"Hi," I said and smiled. "I'm Romaine Wilder—"

"Aren't you Babet's Romaine?" she asked, barely letting me get my words out.

"Yes," I said.

"The doctor?" I nodded. "Oh, please come in," she said.

God bless, Auntie, her popularity could be a big help. I had wondered what I was going to say to Delphine Griffith for her to let me in the door. Now all I needed was a way to get her tell me about the ricin.

"Thank you, Mrs. Griffith," I said, and walked inside the door.

"Oh, please, call me Delphine," she said, "Everyone does."

"Okay, Delphine," I said.

"Come in. Come in," she said. "Sit." She pointed to a chair. "Would you like something to drink? I have tea, juice, coffee. Oh, and bottled water, I know how you young people like bottled water."

Letting her get me something seemed like the right thing to do. And, I thought, keeping her distracted might make it easier to get information from her.

"I'll have a cup of coffee, if it won't be too much trouble," I said, sitting where she'd directed.

"No trouble at all," she said, smiling. "I'll just be a minute."
She scooted off to the kitchen.

I stood up, peeked into the kitchen at her. She had busied
herself making me feel welcomed. I walked around her small living
room, it was cozy and filled with charms. Then I spotted a mum.
"You going to Homecoming?" I asked.

"I'm going to the one at Angel's Grace. Riding over with some
family to see other family." She laughed. "We're going to leave
early, make a few stops on the way. A little day trip for us. A couple
were complaining about leaving so early for an event that doesn't
start until six p.m."

"I was afraid I might be visiting too early," I called after her. "I
wasn't sure if you were an early riser."

"Oh my. Not me. It's ten o'clock," she said from the kitchen.
"Only way I'd still be sleep would be if I were dead."

I laughed. I walked over to the kitchen doorway and poked my
head in. "I'm glad I found you up and healthy."

"Me, too," she said and smiled. She was putting coffee into an
automatic maker.

"Is there anything I can do?" I asked.

"Oh no," she said. "I've got this down to a science. I serve up
coffee all day long."

"All day?"

"Yes. I teach classes here at the house."

"Oh, really?" I said. "What is it that you teach?"

"What else, dear? Herbology."

"Of course," I said.

"I'm not saying anything bad about your profession, mind you,
but knowing natural remedies is very important," she said.

"I agree with that," I said. "Do you get many students?"

"Steady flow," she said. She sat a cup and saucer on the table.
"Come, sit down." I sat. "I teach everyone. Not so many young
people that come, you know they're not having so many aches and
pains quite yet."

I chuckled. "They don't worry about getting sick."

"But what they don't understand is that prevention is worth a pound of cure. Some of my herbs will prevent them from having health problems later on."

"That's true," I said.

"Is that what you tell your patients?"

"It wouldn't help my patients," I said.

"Well, why not?"

"I'm a medical examiner."

"Oh, like Doc Westin." She nodded. "I think I did hear about you taking his place."

"You probably heard that from my auntie." I shook my head. "I'm not taking his place."

"You're not?"

"No. But that is kind of what I came to ask you about," I said.

"Do you want cream and sugar?" she asked as she poured coffee into my cup.

"No thank you," I said. "I like it black."

"I guess it just went right past me that you came here to ask me something. I have a lot of people knocking on my door. You know, coming for herbs and remedies, or to take a class."

"I'm sure," I said. I took a sip of coffee. "Mmmm. This is very good."

"I ground the beans myself," she said. "So, now what was your question?"

"I was wondering if you helped Doc Westin."

She stopped what she was doing and looked at me. "Helped him do what?"

"Well, I know that you grew castor beans, I wondered if he came by to get some from you."

"No. Not the castor beans," she said. "But how did you know about that?"

"My auntie told me that she had asked you to grow them." I took another sip of coffee.

"Oh," she said. "Because she didn't know about the ricin."

"The ricin?" I said. "You gave ricin to Doc Westin?"

"I did."

"Do you know what he did with it?" Of course I knew, I just wondered if she did because his wife had said not many people knew.

"I have no idea. He told me Babet was out of town so he couldn't get any from her, and he'd first tried the only other herbalists he knew."

"Who?"

"The Wilson Twins," she said. "And they told him about me."

"Did he drive out here to get it?"

"Yes, he did."

"I see," I said. My mind was swirling. What did he do with it? Why wasn't any in that container? Had Doc Westin taken it? All of it?

"But I called him and told him that I didn't think the first batch I gave him was good," Delphine Griffith said, spilling more information without any prodding from me. "You know there is a process to extracting it."

"Yes, that's what I understand," I said.

"And I hadn't perfected it the first time."

"You did it twice?"

"Oh, more than that," she said. "I have some in my cabinet now. Would you like to see it?"

"See it?" I shook my head. "No," I said. "I don't want to see it. You know it's very deadly, right?"

"Don't insult me, young lady. Of course I know. But I have it hidden. Right in the back of there," she said and pointed to one of the upper cabinets. "And it's not the only deadly herb I have. I'm sure Babet keeps plenty of them as well."

"Yes, she does," I said. "And I apologize if I upset you."

"You didn't upset me," she said, and smiled. "Why are you looking for ricin?"

"I'm not," I said. "I found a notebook with in Doc Westin's personal things that mentioned it. I just wondered where he might have gotten it from."

"Well now you have your answer," she said and patted my cheek. "He got it from me."

I had to come clean to Auntie. Sneaking around behind her back made me feel guilty. We were supposed to be in this together.

I got back home after one o'clock and Auntie was busy up front. I grabbed a baked chicken out of the fridge and a knife. A chicken sandwich sounded good for lunch.

"What you up to, Sugarplum?" Auntie said. She came into the kitchen just as I was finishing up lunch.

"It's what I've *been* up to," I said. "Thought, I should tell you."

"And what have you been up to?" She got the teapot, filled it up with water and put it on the stove. "Want a cup of tea?"

"Don't need any of your truth serum," I said. "I plan on confessing."

"I was just going to make a little lavender tea. I feel a headache coming on."

"I went to see Mark and Leonard Wilson this morning," I said.

"You did?" she said and went to her spice cabinet.

"But you knew that, right?"

"Yes. And I know that you went to see Delphine Griffith," she said. "If you were planning on telling me that next."

I laughed. "So I didn't need to feel bad about not telling you?" I said.

"It's nice that you thought you should." She smiled. "So what did you learn?"

"Delphine Griffith made several batches of ricin."

"Did she now?" Auntie said. She poured a purple powder into her steeper and placed it inside a cup.

"Yes, she did," I said. "And she gave at least one to Doc Westin."

"What did she do with the other batches?"

"I don't know, although she told me that she has some in her cabinet."

"Cabinet?"

"Kitchen cabinet."

"Oh dear," Auntie said. "She has a lot of people going in and out of her house with the classes she teaches."

"Yeah, so she told me."

"Someone could have taken it."

"A lot of 'someones' could have taken it," I said. "Maybe even some people we hadn't considered."

"So our suspect list just grew?"

"Exponentially."

Chapter Thirty-Nine

Auntie and I pulled into her reserve parking space at Angel's Grace. We were there for the homecoming dinner and awards. That night's annual activity was going to be a little different though—they were going to do a tribute to Bumper.

Jorianne, I'd heard, was going to speak and Boone Alouette and LaJay Reid were going to speak. Mrs. Hackett was going to receive the award for her son. According to Auntie Zanne, it wasn't going to be a somber event, everyone would have on festive mums, smiles on their faces and love in their heart for their friend and loved one."

"I thought you said you made new, less festive ones for this," I said, remember her and Josephine Gail covering the kitchen table, practically kicking me out of the kitchen to redo them.

"I changed my mind," Auntie said. "A girl can do that, you know."

'So, are you the *girl* in this scenario?" I asked.

"That I am," she said and looped her arm through mine.

"Oh, Auntie," I said, leaning down to her. "There's the best man. I didn't think he'd be here."

"He's one of our suspects, isn't he?"

"*Our* suspects?" I asked and chuckled. "He's one of mine."

"We're in this together, kiddo, even though you have been sneaking off doing things without me."

"How about if we go and talk to him?" I said. I didn't want her fussing again about me going to see Delphine Griffith.

"Chase," I said, as we walked toward him. He'd parked farther back in the parking lot and was trying to make his way inside. "I'm surprised to see you here."

"Really?" he said and frowned. "Why shouldn't I be here? I was still in town and this is a tribute to my friend."

"Your friend, huh? From what I've learned you weren't very close with Bumper. I'm wondering how you got to be best man."

"I don't know why that would be any of your business."

"Because we're investigating a murder," Auntie Zanne said. "And you, sir, are a prime suspect."

"Me!" A grin curled up his lip and he shook his head.

"I don't see anything funny," Auntie Zanne said. "Murder is pretty serious business."

"It's laughable to think I killed anyone. That's why I'm here. Michael," he pointed to Auntie Zanne, "Bumper as you call him, was going to help me find out who killed someone I loved."

"What are you talking about?" I said.

"Like I told you before, he had information for me." Chase shook his head. "Maybe I'm being a little over dramatic, but that's how I felt. Michael wanted to help."

"Boy, you're not making one lick of sense," Auntie Zanne said. "You need to just come clean with us. We've got the sheriff on his way."

Of course, that wasn't true. We hadn't even come close to figuring out who it was and had no reason to call Pogue. I guess Auntie just thought that would, as she'd say, light some fire under Chase.

"I don't know what you want to hear," he said, that grin fading from his face.

"How did you know Bumper?" I asked.

"We met out in California. I'm stationed out there as a recruiter."

"Bumper wasn't going into the military," Auntie Zanne said. "He was a sure bet for the NFL."

"I know," he said. "I never said that I was recruiting *him*."

"Just go ahead and finish," I said. I put my hand on Auntie's arm. "Let him talk."

"Well, he's taking forever."

"Go ahead, Chase," I said, ignoring Auntie's comment.

"I was the recruiter at USC. Michael and I struck up a conversation one day and discovered we both were from around the same area."

"Is that why he made you his best man? Because you were a hometown boy?" Auntie just wasn't going to let the boy talk. He was on my suspect list, but Auntie was acting more suspicious of him than I was. "That's the worst lie I've ever heard."

"No," Chase said, "I didn't say that. He made me best man because he made a promise to me and that was his way of showing me he meant it." Chase huffed. "My grandmother..." he closed his eyes and groaned. "My grandmother got this telephone call one day." He shook his head. "It was a scam. These people calling her offering her help with her prescriptions and things and she sent them $500. It was all the money she had and when she found out that she'd been taken, it killed her."

"It killed her?" Auntie asked.

"Not literally, I guess. But that's how I see it. She was so depressed after that. I found out later that that was her bill money for the month. Her grocery money. Everything she had. She didn't want to tell anyone so she just figured she'd suffer through the month and she'd be okay. But she got so sick about it. You know, mentally sick."

"I understand that," Auntie Zanne said. "I have a friend who gets that way. They can just waste away to nothing." That changed Auntie's tone.

"And that's what happened," Chase said. "She died not long after that and I just think it's what killed her. You know, she was sick and old sure, but that scam just seemed to... I don't know. It took her over the edge. But Michael said he might could help me. That maybe he knew something about it. I told him I just wanted those people brought to justice, they shouldn't go messing with old people. He said he agreed. Said he'd 'do the right thing'," he made air quotes, "when he got home."

Chase stuck his hands deep in his pockets. "I didn't believe him though, because he'd come home before, you know after I'd told him about it, and hadn't done it. Said he didn't have the chance to. I told him just to tell me what he knew, and I'd go to the authorities about it. But he didn't want to do that. So this time, he said I could come with him, be his best man, prove to me he was going to do it."

"Your grandmother lived around here?" I asked.

"She lived in Hemphill."

"So why did you lie about not knowing where Bumper's inhaler was?" I asked.

"I didn't say that," he said.

"I asked you had you seen it and you said no."

He shook his head. "No. You asked me did I know what *happened* to it, and I don't. I gave it to that doctor. The one that gave Michael CPR."

"Alex?" I said. "Rather, Dr. Hale?"

"Yeah, that's the name you said when we spoke at the funeral. Dr. Hale." He nodded. "I gave it to Dr. Hale when he followed Michael onto the ambulance."

"You touched it?" Auntie Zanne said. "Did your fingers turn red?"

He looked down at his fingers and rubbed them with his thumb. He hunched his shoulders. "I don't know. I think they were."

"You don't know?" Auntie asked.

"I remember they got red later that night, but I didn't think it had anything to do with that inhaler. I just picked it up and put it in my pocket. Then when I saw Dr. Hale. I gave it to him, told him that Michael might need it."

"And what did he say?" I asked.

"He took it and said okay."

*   *   *

"Well, what do you think about that?" Auntie said as we walked toward Angel's Grace. She glanced back at Chase.

"I think that Chase's grandmother was involved in the same scam that Miriam Colter and some of the other JOY Club members were involved in."

"And Bumper knew who did it?" Auntie Zanne asked.

"Must have known." I dug in my purse and pulled out my phone. "But we've gotta make sure he's telling the truth."

"And how are you going to do that, darlin'?" Auntie Zanne said. "Make him take a polygraph test?"

"What?" I looked at her. "No. I'm going to call Alex and find out if Chase really did give him the inhaler."

"Have you talked to Alex since dinner?" she asked.

"That has nothing to do with this," I said firmly.

"I just think it would be kind of awkward to call him to ask him questions when you haven't discussed your relationship lately."

"There isn't anything wrong with our relationship."

"You sure?"

"Oh goodness, Auntie," I said. "Do you want to investigate this thing or not."

"Go right ahead," she passed her hand in front of me, palm up as if she was serving something up. "I'll just step back," which she did, "and get the tissues ready."

"Who's going to cry?" I asked. "Have you ever seen me cry about Alex?"

"I always have a new travel-size pack of tissues on hand." She patted her handbag.

I ignored her and punched in Alex's number. While it rang I started getting nervous. I glared at Auntie. She was the one making this complicated and me anxious. She was such a troublemaker.

"Hi, Baby," he said. "I was just thinking about you."

Seemed like he was always saying that when I called, yet he didn't call. I guess the thoughts were good enough.

"Hi Alex," I said. I drew in a breath. "Can we talk later? If that's okay."

"Sure. What's going on?"

"Got a question about what happened that day at the house."

"Okay. Shoot."

"Did the best man—a guy in a military uniform—give you an inhaler right before you got into the ambulance?"

"Yeah. He did."

I let out the breath. He had said it so matter-of-factly, no hesitation in his answer. "You sure?" I said, which I knew was ridiculous to ask, he'd just said he had.

"Yeah. Of course," he said. "The guy pulled it out of his pocket and told me Bumper had dropped it when he fell."

"Then what did you do with it?"

"Gave it to the paramedic for him to put with the patient's personal effects. Remember I'd taken off his bowtie when I first started the rescue? And then, at some point we had to get him out of that jacket, too."

"So then what?"

"I intubated him."

"No, I mean with the inhaler."

"It went with him in the ambulance. No one thought he'd been poisoned then, so no reason to do anything special with it," Alex said. "Would have been with all his other stuff."

"Okay," I said.

"Is that all you needed?"

"Yes. I guess that's all."

"Okay. Call me then when you can talk. I'm going back to Chicago tomorrow. I'm not going to get a chance, I don't think, to get back up there."

"It's all right." I paused. "Okay, then. I'll call you."

"Okay, baby. Talk to you soon."

"What did he say?" Auntie said, before I could even click off.

"He said that Chase was telling the truth."

"What does that mean then?" she asked.

I shrugged. "Probably that I should cross Chase Turner off my suspect list."

"Well, that was a waste of time, and now we're running behind," she said. "We've got to get inside."

But then I saw something that stopped me dead in my tracks. "Auntie," I said.

"C'mon, Sugarplum. We gotta hurry."

"Auntie, look," I said and pointed to the back of a black truck."

"What is it?" she said. She kept walking, not even turning around for her inquiry.

"This is the truck that ran me off the road," I called after her.

She turned around, squinted her eyes, and put her hand on her hip. "I thought you said they didn't run you off the road. You hit something and got a flat tire."

"Technically that is what happened," I said. "I guess I exaggerated a little."

"I told you about reigning in your hyperbole," she said and turned around. She waved her hand over her head and waved. "Come on, now. We're late."

I shook my head. That's what I get for lying. I should have told her the truth, I just hadn't wanted her to worry.

I looked at the back of the truck. The fleur-de-lis, it wasn't blue, it was purple. And the yellow was gold. There was an eye in the middle. The tags were from Louisiana and the decal I'd seen across the back window, I had been right, was for the state university.

None of my suspects were from Louisiana.

I wonder where Mighty Max's headquarters are...

Now I just sounded silly.

Chapter Forty

I jotted down the license number. Pogue had no jurisdiction in another state, but I'd have to figure out some way to check it out.

I got to the door, opened it and then stopped. The person who gave me such a scare was inside. Should I go in there? I peeked inside. It was full of people. At least two hundred. That person knew what I looked like, but I didn't know what they looked like.

What if they came to get me...

"Can't decide whether you want to go in or not?"

I turned around, already knowing whose voice it was. It was Rhett.

"I'm considering leaving," I said.

"That might not sit too well with Babet."

"I'm sure it wouldn't," I said.

"Why don't you come in with me?" he said and stuck out the crook of his elbow. "I can escort you in."

"I just saw the truck that was on the road that night you found me at the ME's office." He knew about it, maybe he could help.

"Really," he said, and turned back and looked toward the parking lot. "Who got out of it?"

"I didn't see who it was," I said. "It was already parked when I noticed it."

"So you think the person is in there?" he asked.

"That would be most anyone's logical conclusion."

He laughed. "You're right." He turned again to look at the parking lot. "Maybe you could have your cousin, Pogue, run a check on it."

"It's from Louisiana."

"He can make a call to their state police."

"Or maybe you can make a call to your FBI office?" He knew I was still on the fence about his affiliation with the agency. But that was partly his fault, he never gave me a straight answer.

"Or, I can do that," he said, a sly smile curling around the ends of his lips.

"Yeah, right," I said and stepped inside the door. "I'll be alright." I blew out a breath. "I don't suppose anyone would try to do anything to me in a crowd of two hundred people."

"Didn't stop whoever killed Bumper."

"Thanks for making me feel better," I said.

"Anything I can do to help," he said. He put his hand in the small of my back and leaned down and whispered in my ear, "Don't worry, I'll protect you. I'll stay real close and watch your every move."

"I don't want to put you out," I said.

"Oh, you won't. In case you hadn't noticed, it's what I do all the time."

"What?"

"Watch your every move."

I shook my head and sucked my tongue. "I have to find Auntie," I said, and looked around the room. "I'm sure she needs me to do something."

"I'll come with you," he said.

"There you are!" A voice came toward me.

"Looks like she found you," Rhett said.

Auntie came sashaying across the room. Her navy silk dress shimmering as she walked, her arm filled with bangles and bobbles. Her white hair high in the top, not moving one bit as she moved.

And walking next to her was Delphine Griffith.

"Hi Miss Griffith," I said. She looked at me and squinted her eyes, scolding. "I mean Delphine. What are you doing here?"

"Remember I told you I had family in Roble?" Delphine said.

She smiled at me.

"That's right you did," I said.

"I love to be around when praise is being heaped on family members, or in this case when they are doing the heaping."

"That's nice," Auntie Zanne said.

"If you'll excuse me," she said, looking around. I want to say hello before the program begins."

"Sure," I said.

"That's fine, Delphine," Auntie said. "Romaine can talk to you after the awards ceremony."

"I'd like that," she said.

"Don't be mean to her because she gave me information," I said to Auntie after Delphine left.

"I wasn't being mean. Rhett, was I being mean to her?" Auntie said.

I watched as Delphine made her way over to the back room where the people in the program were getting ready and pop her head in, seemingly waiting for permission to enter.

"C'mon," Auntie said, pulling me and my attention away. "I need to show you something."

"What?" I said. "Can't it wait?"

"No." Her voice dropped to a whisper and she started walking. I guessed I was supposed to follow her.

"Where are we going?" Rhett said.

"You stay here," Auntie said pointing at Rhett. "We'll be right back."

Not moving, I looked over at Rhett. "Why can't he go?"

Auntie grabbed my hand and gave it a yank. "C'mon, I said."

"Can you tell *me* where we're going?"

"I've got a witness to the murder," she said leaning into me.

"You do?"

"Well not to the murder, but to the motive *for* the murder."

"What was the motive for the murder?" I asked.

She huffed. "Really?" She gave my arm another pull to move me along. "Bribery. Gratuities. Conspiracy!" she said.

"Is this about Coach Buddy and Shane Blanchard?"

"Yes," she said. "Who else?"

"Well then why couldn't Rhett come?" I said looking back at him as Auntie dragged me in the back of the community center. "I thought it was his sting operation."

"I'm not so sure about that," she said. "The other day, he made it seem as if I didn't know what I was talking about."

"Maybe he didn't want to break his cover."

But before she got to answer we arrived at the storage closet where she'd stashed the Mighty Max drinks, and it seemed to stop her in her tracks. The door was standing open and there were only half as many cases of the watery blue-filled bottles as there'd been the first time she showed them to me.

"Oh no!" she said.

"What's going on?" I asked.

"I left King Patterson here."

"Who?"

"He's a football player. I'm also tutoring him in algebra so he can get a scholarship and play college ball."

"You're tutoring someone in algebra?" I said, surprised.

"Yes. Why is that surprising? Math is the same as when I was young, I learned it then never forgot it. Now I share what I know. It's what we all should do. But that's not my concern right now."

"I just never thought—"

She grabbed my arm and put one finger up to her lips, telling me to keep quiet. Tilting her head, she seemed to be listening for something.

"Did you hear that?" she asked in a strained whisper.

"No," I said in my regular voice.

"Shhhh!" she said and pulled me away from the closet and toward the back door. It was made out of glass and led out to the back parking lot. She peered through the door, let out a whistle and said, "The nerve! Will you look at that?" And with that she turned, went back to the storage closet and grabbed a broom. I didn't venture over to look out the door, whatever was out there, as far as

I was concerned, could stay. But Auntie had other ideas for me. On the way back she clutched my hand and pulled me out the door behind her.

"What the...!" I said, faltering at her show of strength.

"I gotcha!" Auntie said, pointing her broom at Shane Blanchard who stood in the parking lot behind a truck, the bed filled with the missing cases.

He chuckled when he saw Auntie. "The wicked witch of Roble. Where you off to on your broom?"

"What do you think you're doing?" she said.

"I'm taking back my drinks. You don't seem to want to do anything with them."

"You're not taking those anywhere," she said. "They're evidence."

"Evidence of what?" he said. "Of a booster club president who doesn't know how to take care of the local football team?"

"Football?" she said, her eyes squinting. "Where is King?"

"I'm right here, Mrs. Derbinay," a boy said coming from around the truck.

"What are you doing out here?"

"I was just helping Mr. Blanchard," he said, his eyes were big and he held out his hands like he was pleading. "It's okay, Mrs. Derbinay," he said. "Really it is."

"Leave the boy alone," Shane said. "He doesn't need anything from you, we've got him covered."

"You don't have anything covered," Auntie Zanne said and rushed Shane Blanchard with her broom.

Chapter Forty-One

It took King and I more than a minute or two to subdue Auntie and get the broom from her. King grabbed her around the waist and pulled her away, her feet kicking and her yelling, while I snatched the broom out of her tightly fisted hands. Still we couldn't get Shane Blanchard to leave. Football player King dug up some defensive basketball moves—hands up in air, feet shuffling around Auntie to keep her from attacking Shane again—while I dug my phone out of my purse to call Pogue.

"I'll be back," Shane said. "With lawyers. Those drinks are my property," he shook a fist at us as he drove away. "And you can't keep them."

"Auntie!" I said after hanging up from Pogue. "What in the world was that about? Causing a scene at the banquet. Attacking folks with a broom."

"Those drinks were evidence." Auntie leaned against me, so tired she couldn't hold herself upright. She wiped the sweat from her brow. "And no one saw me back here."

"Still," I said and shook my head.

"I told you Shane Blanchard gave me those cases of that Nasty Max as a bribe so I'd point Roble's football players to him."

"You don't know that for sure."

"I do now," she said, huffing out of breath and pointed to King. "He was my witness. I told you I was going to look into it."

"I still am, Mrs. Derbinay."

"You were helping him take the evidence away," she said,

trying to raise her voice at King, but didn't have enough breath.

"Whether you have the drinks or not, it's not stopping me from telling what I know," King said. "I owe you that as much as you've helped me. And I told you I would." He came over and stood by her, putting his hand in hers. "I just didn't want him to hurt you."

"It looked like she was the one doing all the hurting," I said.

"Well, he better not come back," Auntie Zanne said.

"I've got Pogue on the way," I said.

"What's going on?" It was Rhett. He was standing at the door holding it opened. "Something told me to come back and check on you guys."

"Well something told you too late," I said. "Auntie just attacked Shane Blanchard." I pointed to King. "With a broom." King held it up and wiggled it back and forth.

"Babet," Rhett said and shook his head. "Didn't I tell you to leave that man alone?"

"He's a no good scoundrel and somebody had to do something about it, plus he was stealing my Mighty Max."

"You don't even like that stuff," I said. We started walking back toward the door to Rhett.

"On top of all that," she said once we got inside, "he's the killer."

"Killer?" Rhett asked.

"She thinks he killed Bumper," I said.

"Mr. Blanchard killed Bumper?" King asked. "Oh man!"

"We don't know that," I said.

"I do," Auntie said. "He and Coach Buddy."

"Oh yeah, I'm definitely telling on them," King said. "Bumper was a legend around here."

"I guess he is now that he's dead," Auntie Zanne said. She looked at King. "I'm sorry you had to see that. But that man is hurting my boys."

"It's okay," he said. "I only helped him so he wouldn't hurt you, but I see you don't really need any back up."

Auntie shook her head and blew out a breath. "We'd better get started," she said and nodded her head toward the front of the center.

"Don't you want to wait until Pogue gets here so you can make a report?" I asked.

"No," Auntie Zanne said. "I can do it after the banquet. King's right, I don't need that Deadly Max drink to get Shane Blanchard if I've got King. And trust me, he's going to get it for trying to interfere in my boys' hopes of going to school and playing ball."

"And for killing Bumper?" Rhett said, a smirk on his face, I knew he was just egging her on.

"That's not funny," I said. "You see how out of control she gets."

Rhett chuckled. We made it back up to the front, and I stopped Auntie, straightened out her clothes and puffed her hair back up. "We don't want anyone to know you were having schoolyard fights out back," I said. "Now lick your lips and put on a smile."

She did as she was told and smiled back at me. "I'm okay," she said, and gave a firm nod. "I'll just go in and check on my dais so we can get this started.

As she started over, I saw Miriam Colter slip into the room right ahead of her.

Then something clicked inside my head.

I looked over at Auntie. She was waltzing toward the room, arm outstretched to reach for the knob, my eyes wide as saucers, my jaw slack.

Oh, my gosh, I thought and took in a breath, *I know who killed Bumper!*

"Auntie, stop!" I said rather loudly across the room. "Don't go in that room."

"What?" Auntie Zanne said, turning to look at me. She placed her hand on the doorknob. "Don't worry. I'll be right back out."

"No! We have to wait to start, Auntie," I said, I trotted over to her and pulled her hand away. "We can't start until Pogue gets here."

"I already told you, I'll make the report later."

"I don't understand why he isn't here," I said, turning to look out of the front doors. "What is taking him so long?" I pulled out my phone to call him again.

"I think everything will be okay," Rhett said. "Shane's gone, I don't think he'll be back after what you said Babet did."

"Why are you looking so worried?" Auntie said.

I was fumbling with the phone and mumbling. "He came to the funeral," I muttered. "He should've been here, too."

"He came to the funeral to find the killer, which he evidently didn't do because he just left here with a truck full of evidence. And neither did we..." Auntie was still rambling when Pogue picked up the line.

"Pogue," I said whispering into the phone. I wasn't sure if the butterflies were from me solving it, or fear of how my poor cousin was going to react when I told him I had.

"Romie, why are you whispering into the phone? Are you alright? I thought everything was under control."

"I thought you were on your way here. How far away are you from Angel's Grace?"

"Why? What's wrong?"

"I think I may have solved the case, and the killer is here now."

"What case, Romie? You better not be talking about the Hackett case. I thought this was just missing sports drinks."

I grunted. "Okaaay..."

"What case, Romie?"

"Uhm..."

"Romie."

"The Hackett case." I spit it out. "I've solved the Hackett case."

Auntie Zanne looked at me, surprise in her eyes. Rhett shook his head and started grinning.

"I knew it!" Auntie Zanne said. "I was right all along."

"It's not who you think," I told her.

"You did what?" Pogue said. He was yelling into my ear.

"I'm not right?" Auntie Zanne said, yelling into the other one. "Who is it then? How do you know who did it?"

"Shhh!" I said to Auntie Zanne, "I can't hear Pogue."

"I told you not to go messing in my case," Pogue said.

"Well if you don't get over here soon, that statement is going to come back and bite you in the butt because I have solved it and you're going to let the killer get away."

Chapter Forty-Two

It seemed like it took forever for Pogue to get to the community center and I was a little nervous about people getting restless or anxious. But deep down I knew that people around these parts did whatever Auntie Zanne wanted, so her saying we had to delay didn't cause any commotion. Most people thought that if Babet Derbinay said it was necessary, it must be. And she posted her Roble Belles to the outside door, and told the twins, Mark and Leonard Wilson to guard the door where I told her the killer was. She was going to make sure no one got away.

I had filled Auntie in on who I thought the killer was right after I spoke with Pogue. She didn't want to wait for Pogue to get there so I wouldn't have to tell the story twice, she had to know right then.

"I'm not holding up this event unless you tell me," she had said. "I have to know what you've come up with is legit."

Certainly because her suspect was "legit."

I shook my head. I needed her to help me contain the situation, so I spilled the beans and told her my theory. Rhett found out because, true to his word, he didn't leave my side.

"Well, I'll be a monkey's uncle," she said when I told her. "That's sounds like it could be right."

When Pogue got there, looking very official and stern, but not as infuriated as I thought he'd be. He came in and walked over to me.

"Auntie Zanne has everyone contained," I pointed to the back room. "So I can give you a quick rundown and you can go in."

He held up his hand to stop me when I tried to tell him how I'd figured it out and said, "Let's just do this. You can tell me once we get in there." He started walking toward the room.

"But wait," I said, and caught up with him. "We need to get another person in that room."

"Why?"

"Because he needs to be in there."

He huffed. "Who is it?"

I pointed with my head. "That guy over there."

Pogue turned and looked at the direction I was pointing. "I've seen him before," he said. "At the funeral."

"Right," I said. "He was also the best man at the wedding."

"What's his name?"

"Chase Turner."

"Fine. I'll get him. Then are we good to go into the room?"

I nodded.

"Okay." He looked over at Rhett. "Can you come back there, too? I might need your help."

"Sure," Rhett said. "Happy to help."

Pogue collected Chase without too much disruption and we relieved the Wilson Twins of their post. I wasn't sure how much resistance they could put up if anyone had tried to exit, but Auntie Zanne must have felt confident in their abilities.

When we walked in, everyone turned to look at us. Everyone included the wedding party: Piper, Marilee, Tonya, Boone, and LaJay. Chase hadn't been invited to participate in the tribute so he wasn't in the back but I knew that he too was on lock down and wouldn't be able to escape.

Then there was Mrs. Hackett, Mrs. Alvarez, Delphine Griffith and Miriam Coulter. Those last two entering the room was what tipped me off to the identity of the murderer.

I was pretty sure at this point the culprit had thought that no one was on their trail.

"Are we ready to start?" Mrs. Hackett asked when we came in.

She seemed impatient. There was sweat over her upper lip smearing her flat red lipstick.

"Not quite yet," Auntie Zanne said. "Pogue needs to speak with you first."

"Sheriff Folsom," I leaned in and whispered to Auntie.

"What?" she said and frowned. "Oh yes," she nodded acknowledging my correction. "I meant Sheriff Folsom. He's here on official business."

"What kind of official business?" Piper asked.

"Murder," Pogue said.

"I'm just here because I'm in charge of the mums," Miriam Colter said. "I haven't killed anyone lately."

"Lately?" Pogue asked.

"Did I say lately?" Mrs. Colter said. "I meant ever." She fanned her face and blew out a breath. "Never."

"Same goes for me," Delphine Griffith said. "I just came to say hi to Boone." She looked at him and smiled sweetly. "He's that family I told you about." She directed her last statement to me.

"I know," I said and nodded.

"Okay," Pogue said. "Let's do this." He turned to me. "Romaine," he said and snorted. "You do it. Tell them."

I could tell he was upset with me, not mad, but I wasn't going to try to placate him in front of everybody in the room. Plus, I was happy to tell what I'd discovered.

"Tell us what?" Mrs. Alvarez said. I didn't think she thought very highly of me after I sat with her at the funeral.

"Who Bumper's murderer is," Auntie said. "She's figured it out."

All eyes turned to me.

"Have you?" Mrs. Hackett asked. "You know who killed my son?"

"I do," I said.

"And who was it?" Mrs. Hackett said. "Are they in this room?"

I nodded. "Yes. He is in this room. Waiting to go out and speak about your son like nothing happened. Aren't you, Boone?"

"Boone!" His name came from several places around the room. "No!" I heard someone else say among the gasps.

"When did you come up with that craziness?" Boone asked. "I didn't do anything."

"Oh, but you did," I said. "I just figured it out today. When I saw your truck." I looked at Auntie. "What division one school recruited Boone Alouette, Auntie Zanne? Do you know?"

"Oh, I sure do," she said. "Lots of them wanted him, but he chose Louisiana State University. Didn't you, Boone?"

"So?" he said.

"So that was one of the things that helped me figure it was you," I said. "No, it wasn't the smoking gun, but it wasn't until I saw it today that I could put all the pieces together."

"Today?" he said narrowing his eyes.

"Yes," I said, a smirk spreading across my face. "But that's not what you thought, is it? You thought I was on to you a lot earlier than just today, didn't you?" I said.

"I don't know what you're talking about," he said, his attitude nonchalant, his words flat.

"Oh, I think you do," I said. "Yours was the truck that tried to run me over the other night out by the morgue."

"No it wasn't," he said.

"The purple and gold fleur-de-lis decal on the bumper." I let my words linger before I continued. "Louisiana State University lettering in your back window."

"If I was behind the wheel and wanted you dead, you would be," he said.

"Just like you wanted Bumper dead?" Auntie said.

"What reason would I want that?" Boone asked and shrugged. "He was my best friend."

"Your best friend who didn't want you as a best man," she countered.

"I told you, just like I told everyone," Boone answered, agitation bubbling up, "I wasn't sure I could get here."

"He didn't want you as his best man because he knew what

you'd been up to," I said.

"You're sounding crazy," Boone said, I was sure he had no idea I'd figured out all of it. "I haven't been up to anything."

"You've been up to a lot," Auntie Zanne said.

"Like what?" Mrs. Alvarez said. She certainly didn't seem so bothered with me any more.

"Like scamming old people out of their savings in a Medicare scam," Auntie Zanne said. She just wasn't going to let me tell anything without her input.

"Medicare scam?" Boone bit down on his bottom lip, his eyes darting around the room.

Yeah, Boone, we got you...

"You moved from credit cards to Medicare, didn't you?"

I wasn't so sure about that, but Bumper had promised Chase a confession and that was the only motive I could think of as I was sure it was Boone who had killed him.

"Wait," a voice came from the door. I turned to look and it was Chase.

"We didn't ask you in here to interrupt," Pogue said to Chase. "Keep it up and you're going to have to leave."

"No. I know about this," Chase said, his words stumbling out. He looked to me pleadingly, seemingly asking for me to get him permission to speak. "He's the one Bumper was going to tell me about." He squinted his eyes and shook his head. "I-Isn't that what you're saying?"

"Yes," I said. "That's what I'm saying. Bumper had promised you he would get a confession for you from the guilty party. That was you, right, Boone?"

"He wasn't going to make me tell anyone anything," Boone said defiantly. "Who did he think he was? He wasn't no angel."

"Don't talk about the dead," Mrs. Alvarez said and came and stood next to Mrs. Hackett.

"Hold on." Miriam Colter used her cane to push herself up from the chair. "Is Boone the one that called my house?"

"Possibly," I said. "But if he isn't, I'm almost sure he can tell you it was."

"What does this have to do with murder, Romaine?" Pogue said.

"It's the motive, Pogue," I said, not taking my eyes off of Boone. "And it's the reason that Bumper didn't want Boone to be his best man."

"I already told you... I told everyone," Boone's anger was starting to bare, "I wasn't sure if I could get here."

"You knew you could," I said, "He didn't want you because of the bad things you'd done. Hurting people and not wanting to fess up. And you were afraid if you didn't confess, he would tell. So that's when you came up with your plan."

"What?" he said and hunched his shoulders. "What did I plan?"

"The murder." I heard another collective gasp. "You killed Bumper because he was going to tell that you were part of that Medicare scheme that bilked money from seniors. You used their need to get help with their Medicare Part D plans. Telling them to send you money and they wouldn't have to ever pay for prescriptions again."

"Let me at him," Miriam said, waving her cane. "He'll need more than Medicare when I finish with him."

"Somebody want to get her?" Pogue said.

"I've got her," Delphine said, patting Mrs. Colter on the back. "C'mon now, let them take care of this."

"What was my murderous plan?" Boone said. "Bet you can't answer that. You know why? Because there wasn't one."

"Oh, yes it was, and I can answer that," I said. "The first part of your plan was to trigger an asthma attack to make sure Bumper needed an inhaler. He hadn't had an episode in a long time, since he moved to California." I could see Mrs. Hackett nodding her head. "So you planned a trip to Louisiana. You knew taking Bumper to Lake Charles, one of the most humid places in the south, after he'd spent so much time in L.A. would trigger an asthma attack."

"There's a lot of humidity in Lake Charles?" Mrs. Hackett

asked. Her face contorted, she was wringing her hands.

"It is," I said.

"How would I know that?" Boone said.

"Because you go to school in Baton Rouge," Auntie Zanne chimed in, her tone sarcastic. "You had to know how humid it was Louisiana, especially near water."

"You knew that was his trigger," Jorianne said, repeating my already mentioned observation. "Is that why you wanted to keep it a secret?" She got more upset with each word. "Where you were taking him? Upset because he posted those pictures of the Golden Nugget?"

"No," Boone said. "I didn't think about that. None of this makes sense. How would I have even killed him?"

"You put poison in his inhaler," Auntie Zanne said.

"I did not!"

"Yes, you did," I said. "In the inhaler that you told me you hadn't seen."

"I didn't see it," Boone said. "And Piper told you that Chase had it. He's probably the one who did it." He flung an arm toward Chase. "We don't even know anything about him."

"Oh, Chase did have Bumper's inhaler," I said. "The one he used in the gazebo that day. But he gave it to Dr. Hale when he was going into the ambulance." I looked at Pogue. "He can verify that's what happened."

"That is what happened," Chase said.

"And I bet if we test Chase's military uniform pants pocket, where he put it after he picked it up when Bumper collapsed, we might even find traces of the poison he used to kill him."

"How'd Boone get hold of an inhaler?" Pogue asked, coming to stand next to me.

"I'm sorry to say it, but Mrs. Hackett had them strategically placed everywhere." I glanced over at her. "She had even passed them out to the wedding party."

"He was having trouble breathing," Mrs. Hackett said. "I didn't want... I didn't know..." She broke out in sobs. Piper went over and rubbed her back. "I didn't want anything to happen to him," she blurted. Her eyes were red-rimmed. "I wanted to have his medicine close by."

"And Boone counted on you doing that," I said. "That way he wouldn't have to worry about it being suspicious that he had an inhaler."

"Boone asked me did I have any around," Mrs. Hackett said.

"When?" I asked.

"After he came home from school for the wedding." She sniffed. "He thought maybe the nervousness of the day might trigger an attack. Said he just wanted to careful."

"Boone said that to you?" Jorianne said.

She nodded, she was trying to hold back more tears so she could speak. "Asked me if I still put them all around."

"I did no such thing," Boone said.

"Yes, you did," Mrs. Hackett said.

"What did you tell him?" Auntie Zanne asked.

"I told him yes. But they probably weren't any good after all this time. Still that made me think I should get more."

"How did you get them?" I asked, remembering that Mr. McDougal at the pharmacy said he hadn't seen a prescription for Bumper since he left for college.

"Miriam Coulter," Mrs. Hackett said and pointed.

We looked over at her. She held up her hands in defense. "Didn't I just say I hadn't killed anyone?"

"You gave Mrs. Hackett inhalers?" I asked.

"Yes. They were for him. Doc Westin had ordered some for Mrs. Hackett when Bumper left for college. I just got some of those."

The box, I thought. There were inhalers in the box where the ricin was.

"Did you bother anything else in the box?"

"In the box?" she said and squinted. "Did you go through them? I packed them up for Mrs. Westin's eyes, not anyone else's."

"Just answer the question, Miriam," Auntie Zanne said. "We

don't have time for your monkey business."

"No. Didn't touch anything else. Got the inhalers and gave them to Mrs. Hackett."

"And I passed them out," Mrs. Hackett said, she nodded toward Boone. "He was the first person I gave one to. Before they even left for their trip."

"Oh," I said, the realization hitting me that maybe Bumper never had a real asthma attack. That he might have been reacting to ricin the entire time. "Is that when you first gave Bumper the poison? When you were in Lake Charles?"

"I told you, I don't know what you're talking about," Boone said.

"Wait," Pogue said. "Let's just back up for a minute here. You were talking about the inhaler at the wedding. That's the one that we know for sure had poison on it, right?"

"Right," I said.

"So where is that one?" Pogue asked.

"Chase gave it to Alex," I said. "Alex gave it to the paramedics who put it with Bumper's things, and then Boone got it when he was at the hospital."

"He wanted to dispose of the evidence," Auntie Zanne said.

"That's a convoluted passing around of a murder weapon," Pogue said. "Might be a problem with chain of custody."

"But it's what happened," I said.

"Is that what you did?" Mrs. Hackett asked, realization hitting her, she sniffed back her tears. "When we were at the hospital? You came back with his jacket and bowtie. Did you get the inhaler while you were back there, too?"

That sent Boone into a tailspin. He turned around in circles and grabbed his head. His face had turned beet red and he eyes were filled with tears. "You don't know what you're talking about!" he boomed, spit spewing as he yelled. "I didn't do anything!"

"What kind of poison was it?" Piper asked.

"Ricin," I said, having to speak over Boone's wailing. Then as I spoke, along with Boone's cries came another shriek. At first I thought it was Miriam Colter, attempts to keep her down perhaps unsuccessful, and she'd let out a war cry. But it was Delphine Griffith.

"Boone Alouette!" she screeched. "Did you take that from my house? Ricin!" She stood up and shook her fist at him. "I shared what it was with you and then you stole from me? I knew I had some missing. I knew I had more in my cabinet."

"How would you know some was missing?" Boone said. "As much as you had up there. Anyone could have gotten some of it."

She grabbed the air like she was holding on to his collar and gave it a push. "You used it to kill somebody? My own flesh and blood using God's bounty for evil!"

"I don't know what you're talking about," he barked at her. "Don't say something like that. Don't say that now!"

"Is this what you do with the knowledge I give you?" She shook her head back and forth with such vigor I thought she'd given herself something akin to shaken baby syndrome. "You are no kin of mine!" she cried.

That seemed to bother him. "I'm not saying anything," Boone said. He wiped his face with the back of his hand, sniffed back his tears, then crossed his arms. "I know that I am supposed to have a lawyer."

"Fine, you want a lawyer. They can come down to the jail to talk to you. I've heard enough," Pogue said pulling handcuffs out of his back pocket. "Turn around, Boone. I'm placing you under arrest for the murder of Michael Hackett."

Epilogue

Auntie insisted that the Roble Homecoming Award Dinner proceed *sans* Boone. Bumper still deserved it so everyone needed to close their slack jaws, still open at the surprise of Boone being the murderer and put on a smile. It was time to start.

In the days that followed, Pogue wouldn't take my phone calls, and he seemed to be out of the office every time I called. I didn't mean to hurt my cousin. I didn't know how far he'd gotten in his investigation, and even after he started speaking to me again, he wouldn't tell me.

I decided that I loved investigating, even if it made my cousin angry with me. It made me feel useful and needed. And, I discovered, it gave me a chance to spend time with Auntie. I knew that was what she wanted.

Boone ended up taking a plea. As far as the Medicare scheme, he didn't speak about it. Miriam Counter had taken care of it by getting her brother-in-law, who was a retired federal judge, to make some calls on her behalf and whatever they came up with seemed to factor into Boone's decision.

But mostly it was Delores Hackett.

At first, Boone wouldn't admit to anything—the scam or murder. He wouldn't even talk to the lawyer he said he wanted, but he changed his mind after a visit from Mrs. Hackett. No one knew what she'd said to him, neither one of them would tell. So, he took a plea—life without the possibility of parole instead of a death sentence like the Texas judicial is so fond of giving.

And, as for me, there wasn't as much talking behind closed doors and I was in a state of confusion about it.

I didn't know what to do about Alex or Rhett.

Alex thought everything was fine between the two of us—nothing had changed. He still planned for us to be together just like we'd talked about before I left Chicago. Only I wasn't sure that's what I wanted anymore.

But did I want Rhett? Better question, did Rhett want me? Because if he did, why was he flaunting another woman in front of me?

Or was he?

Hailey Aaron had popped out of sight just as quickly she had popped in, and Rhett hadn't said anything about her.

Auntie Zanne had said, even though I hadn't mentioned one word to her about it, that if I wanted to know who she was to Rhett, I should ask.

And Shane Blanchard and Coach Buddy Budson were indicted, yep, lo and behold Auntie Zanne was right, they were running a gratuity and bribery operation. LaJay Reid wasn't implicated, but they seemed to refer to him in the indictment papers that Auntie somehow secured. But to her dismay, it wasn't her "Secret Agent Man," Rhett Remmiere who ran the sting, although to placate her he'd made a call to see if any operations had their sights on the two. They, along with a few other conspirators, had charges filed out of the Washington D.C. Circuit.

I found myself thinking less and less about going back to Chicago and more and more about taking Doc Westin's job. Oh yeah, and making some friends.

ABBY L. VANDIVER

Wall Street Journal Bestselling Author, Abby L. Vandiver, loves a good mystery. Born and raised in Cleveland, it's even a mystery to her why she has yet to move to a warmer place. Abby loves to travel and curl up with a good book or movie. A former lawyer and college professor, she has a bachelor's degree in Economics, a master's in Public Administration, and a Juris Doctor. Writer-in-Residence at her local library, Abby spends all of her time writing and enjoying her grandchildren.

**The Romaine Wilder Mystery Series
by Abby Vandiver**

SECRETS, LIES, & CRAWFISH PIES (#1)
LOVE, HOPES, & MARRIAGE TROPES (#2)

Henery Press Mystery Books

And finally, before you go...
Here are a few other mysteries
you might enjoy:

FIXIN' TO DIE

Tonya Kappes

A Kenni Lowry Mystery (#1)

Kenni Lowry likes to think the zero crime rate in Cottonwood, Kentucky is due to her being sheriff, but she quickly discovers the ghost of her grandfather, the town's previous sheriff, has been scaring off any would-be criminals since she was elected. When the town's most beloved doctor is found murdered on the very same day as a jewelry store robbery, and a mysterious symbol ties the crime scenes together, Kenni must satisfy her hankerin' for justice by nabbing the culprits.

With the help of her Poppa, a lone deputy, and an annoyingly cute, too-big-for-his-britches State Reserve officer, Kenni must solve both cases and prove to the whole town, and herself, that she's worth her salt before time runs out.

Available at booksellers nationwide and online

Visit www.henerypress.com for details

BOARD STIFF

Kendel Lynn

An Elliott Lisbon Mystery (#1)

As director of the Ballantyne Foundation on Sea Pine Island, SC, Elliott Lisbon scratches her detective itch by performing discreet inquiries for Foundation donors. Usually nothing more serious than retrieving a pilfered Pomeranian. Until Jane Hatting, Ballantyne board chair, is accused of murder. The Ballantyne's reputation tanks, Jane's headed to a jail cell, and Elliott's sexy ex is the new lieutenant in town.

Armed with moxie and her Mini Coop, Elliott uncovers a trail of blackmail schemes, gambling debts, illicit affairs, and investment scams. But the deeper she digs to clear Jane's name, the guiltier Jane looks. The closer she gets to the truth, the more treacherous her investigation becomes. With victims piling up faster than shells at a clambake, Elliott realizes she's next on the killer's list.

Available at booksellers nationwide and online

Visit www.henerypress.com for details

MURDER ON A SILVER PLATTER

Shawn Reilly Simmons

A Red Carpet Catering Mystery (#1)

Penelope Sutherland and her Red Carpet Catering company just got their big break as the on-set caterer for an upcoming blockbuster. But when she discovers a dead body outside her house, Penelope finds herself in hot water. Things start to boil over when serious accidents threaten the lives of the cast and crew. And when the film's star, who happens to be Penelope's best friend, is poisoned, the entire production is nearly shut down.

Threats and accusations send Penelope out of the frying pan and into the fire as she struggles to keep her company afloat. Before Penelope can dish up dessert, she must find the killer or she'll be the one served up on a silver platter.

Available at booksellers nationwide and online

Visit www.henerypress.com for details

A MUDDIED MURDER

Wendy Tyson

A Greenhouse Mystery (#1)

When Megan Sawyer gives up her big-city law career to care for her grandmother and run the family's organic farm and café, she expects to find peace and tranquility in her scenic hometown of Winsome, Pennsylvania. Instead, her goat goes missing, rain muddies her fields, the town denies her business permits, and her family's Colonial-era farm sucks up the remains of her savings.

Just when she thinks she's reached the bottom of the rain barrel, Megan and the town's hunky veterinarian discover the local zoning commissioner's battered body in her barn. Now Megan's thrust into the middle of a murder investigation—and she's the chief suspect. Can Megan dig through small-town secrets, local politics, and old grievances in time to find a killer before that killer strikes again?

Available at booksellers nationwide and online

Visit www.henerypress.com for details

CPSIA information can be obtained
at www.ICGtesting.com
Printed in the USA
LVHW041557200220
647644LV00010B/806